# Untamed

# Desire

# La Redeaux

**Untamed Desire**

This is a work of fiction. Names, characters, businesses, places, events and incidents are either the products of the author's imagination or used in a fictitious manner. Any resemblance to actual persons, living or dead, or actual events is purely coincidental.

Published by Midnight Publications
Written by: LaRedeaux
Editing: The Write Way
ISBN-13: 978-0989119580
ISBN-10: 0989119580
LCCN: 2014932610

# Acknowledgements

First I would like to thank everyone that has read a book by me (LaRedeaux).

Special thank you's to the sexy men and women you know who you are…

♥ *Thank you for your purchase, I hope I have reignited your Passion, Lust & Love!* ♥

Pick up other reads by LaRedeaux at
www.midnightpublications.com

These Erotic Short Stories will tantalize your steamy reading needs and fill you with yearning and fantasy. Each sensual story is written to entice your need for a romantic night with your significant other(s). Leave your worries behind and let the sensual reading begin.

This book is not meant for the prude, unless you're willing. For those unafraid to release your sexual tensions and let your ravenous, animalistic desires come forth, Please; enter the *Red Zone!*

## THE WEEKEND: Damaris and Bernard

Concentrating on work has been a very hard task for Damaris ever since her new co-worker, Bernard entered the scene. Her vivid fantasies of him have a profound effect on their working relationship. Will Damaris resist the temptation? Can Bernard fulfill her sexual desires?

## TOUCHDOWN: Torrence and Kashauna

Kashauna loves the Atlanta Falcons as much as any football fan could. However, every year when the season rolls around, her husband thinks, eats, breathes The Falcons. Every year during football season Kashauna experience a sexual drought. This year she devised a plan that will satiate her every desire. Torrence won't know what hit him.

### DESIRE: Safiya and Mike

Desire is the feeling that accompanies an unsatisfied state. Safiya Blue enjoys the view from the top. Ever since she bumped in to Michael Wright at the neighborhood Farmer's Market, she's been longing to fulfill her desire to have him. With a twist of fate and a granted contract, Safiya and Mike will see more of each other. Will they be able to come to terms with their desires or will regulations drench the flame?

### HOUSE OF CHOO: Daemon and Wynda

Wynda Blackwell has two passions, SHOES and SEX. After her husband passes away unexpectedly, she becomes a lonely maiden living in a house of shoes, Jimmy Choo. All she has are shoes and time until sexy handy man Daemon unconsciously ignites her sexual desires, again. This little fairytale will incite your needs for red shoe sex.

## STEAM BATH: Chase and Nasha feat. Marie

She's back! Yes, Marie Scott is more than the housewife she appears to be. After her secrets were cast into the light, she decided to live. Fulfilling desires of herself and everyone she meets, Nasha becomes her newest target. Chase can't seem to break his need for domination and Marie is all too willing to oblige. Nasha has a crush on her handsome trainer, just like many of the other women in her fitness class. Nasha lets her self-consciousness flee after one class.

## DESIRE UNLEASHED: Morgan and Craig

Physical scars can keep a woman's desire restrained. Morgan Clark spends most of her time alone and seeking self-fulfillment. After overhearing her co-workers talk about their new toys, Morgan embarks on a solo flight. Craig Mack recently moved into his grandmother's old apartment and almost immediately after, he hears his shy neighbor. After hearing a large commotion from her apartment Craig's scars might be healed as well.

**Untamed Poetry** is a collection of some of my innermost erotic feelings. Some were inspired by very dear friends and the conversations we've had.

If you're really ready: Enter the *Red Zone!* Enjoy

*LaRedeaux*

# TABLE OF CONTENTS

## Untamed Poetry

*My Love*

*My Fire*

*Seduction*

*Passionately*

*Dark Side*

# The Weekend

Aftermath, the outcome of an event especially as relative to an individual.

Damaris spent the last two weeks dealing with the reactions between her body and her new co-worker Bernard. Somehow, he ended up in her bed, naked and satiated. She watched him sleep in the morning sunlight with the sheet barely covering his gloriously naked body. She laid awake and stared at him while reminiscing on all the devious things they did. She noticed how his bald head shimmered in the sunlight, surrounding him in a natural glow.

She slowly pulled on the high thread-count sheet and watched as the blue sheet cascades over his coffee body. Inch by inch, the sheet revealed a body of hardened muscles and silky skin that just begged for her hands to roam once again. By the time the sheet was almost done uncovering what she was certain was a morning sex dream that had him hard under the sheet his head rolled in her direction, and a sexy smile crept across his delicious lips.

"Morning." His deep baritone voice whispered as his dark eyes slowly adjusted to the sunlight.

"Good morning." Damaris whispered in a flirtatious voice as her hand slowly pulled the last of the sheet aside.

Her eyes twinkled with mischief as the memory of the previous night's escapade flooded her brain with a sensual overload of information. Just the memory of it shimmied on her skin as an erotic reminder.

Her naked body crawled to his body and she straddled him. Positioning herself on his ripped abs, she looked down at him with her oval eyes and smiled wickedly. Her freshly coiffed bob with extended bangs streaked with blond highlights cascaded over her face.

"Last night was fun." She teased knowing his dick wanted nothing more than to enter her wet pussy once again.

"Fun? More like a fantasy come true." He spoke with a fervent tone.

She felt his hardness rubbing against her ass while she straddled him. She could tell that he didn't want to have to ask and she wasn't going to make him. Reaching for the foil packet on the nightstand, she ripped it open with her teeth. With expert precision, she reached behind her back and she let her fingers slowly wrap around his hard dick as she slid the condom on.

She raised herself up, scoot back a spell, and lowered herself onto him. Leaning forward, her streaked hair tickled his forehead. With her hands placed on either side of his head, she whispered, "Last night, you made it all about me and now that I get a turn, I think I'll try on top."

"You can try whatever you like." He teased; his voice was deep and sensual.

The condom was on and his hard dick was in place. "Fuck me!" He pleaded as the seconds passed.

She taunted him, "Promise me this won't end tonight."

"I promise." Bernard's raspy voice said.

Although she would bet he would say anything to have her tight, wet, pussy lower onto his dick. She did the same last night. She moaned in pleasure, asked for things that made him smile wickedly, and made promises of desire to come. Damaris decided she wouldn't make him wait much longer, even though he made her wait several weeks before showing her the physical attention she desired.

She lowered her hips as he slid his dick inside her wet, waiting pussy. Morning sex always had a magical feel to it. A hell of a way to start the morning, it was as if nothing about the day could go wrong. That magical feeling was illuminating her face with a smile followed by soft moans of delight. She let the slickness guide him in and out while she raised and lowered her hips matching his rhythm.

Her movements were slow and easy as his hands gently caressed her breasts all the while looking into her face with a soft smitten smile. He was enjoying this as much as she was, but like the sex the night before slow and easy was not her pace. The reaction her body had for this man was explosive, and she could feel the frenzy building.

She sat up tall, thrust her breasts out, arched her back, and tilted her head to the ceiling as she moaned. "Yes! God, your dick feels so good."

Bernard's hands caressed her as she raised and lowered herself matching his pace. His fingers dipped into the wet folds of her pussy and found her swollen clitoris. He rubbed her gently and she heard his voice filter up to her with a possessiveness that warmed her heart.

"You're so beautiful, so damn sexy on my dick. I could wake up to you every morning like this."

She just bet he could, but working together was one thing, fucking his brains out was another. With each sensual stroke of his dick in her pussy, his fingers rubbing her clitoris, and her own hands pinching her nipples, Damaris wasn't thinking about work or living together. She was thinking how damn good this reaction is to his body and how she felt.

"I'm gonna cum!" She moaned as her body vibrated with a pulsation from her core to every fiber in her being. She trembled and fell down, her breast landed against him. He whispered in her ear while his hands stroked her back.

"So beautiful, so fucking fantastic!" The caress of his hands on her back in a loving motion was tender, but she knew he was not done yet. Her body tried to resolve some type of normalcy to its being.

Damaris rolled off Bernard and assumed the position. She lay on her belly, put her hands under her face, and propped her ass up in the air.

"I know you're not done."

Her wicked smile of offering had him behind her, on his knees, and sliding his anaconda back into her pussy. Bernard grasped her hips in his hands and the morning sun cascading through the bedroom curtains onto his face looked erotic as she stared at him over her shoulder. She adored the love faces he made when his pole entered her. She was so tight from her recent orgasm and so excited from his passionate desire to finish this off for him.

Bernard's thrusts got harder and faster. Damaris listened to the sounds of their skin smacking against each other. His groans were intense and throaty, his teeth clenched and he slammed into her one final time. Hips were thrust forward and his face was to the ceiling. Damaris saw the euphoric look of pleasure on his face, the same one she saw a few times the previous night. It caused her to wonder if this passionate reaction they explored would be one he would be interested in recreating.

His body finally fell on hers and slowly she lowered herself onto the bed. His belly was on her back, but he kept his elbows propped up to keep him from crushing her. His first words told her that this was not going to end here today.

"Damn baby. You really know how to please a guy who's got a crush on you."

Damaris spoke into her pillow with her head turned to the side to look at him. "You had a crush on me?"

He rolled off her and simultaneously she rolled sideways facing him. Bernard turned his head and looked at her with passion in his eyes. "Yeah, since the second I met you; then when you asked me for drinks last night after work, I thought hell yeah. I never would've guessed all this."

"Mmm. Well, it doesn't have to end here. How about, since I technically asked you out last night. You get the next one, deal?"

"Deal!" He spoke with a happiness that filled her heart.

He rolled out of her bed and started for her shower. He stopped short and turned with a devilish look.

"Tonight! My place! Seven, no make it six. An early home-cooked meal and then… Well, you decide. Lady's choice."

That last sentence had Damaris' wicked mind thinking up all kinds of delicious ideas and positions. The memory of him eating her pussy like a fat man at the Golden Coral buffet, told her that option was first on her list.

Damaris heard the sound of the shower running, she thought of joining him, but her body buzzed from everything that was happening. Damaris' mind reeled on how their next encounter would play out. She unconsciously touched herself and her body reacted to her own touch.

The slickness of her skin felt divine. She let her fingers roam like Bernard's did prior to sensual foreplay. He was so tender and sweet until she demanded more from him. She liked her sex with men a lot of ways, but with the way her body reacted since cast of his piercing eyes, she knew she needed it hard and rough.

Damaris massaged herself between her thighs and separated her engorged pussy lips to find her clitoris sensitive from her touch. She massaged herself up and down, and back and forth with her fingertips. Each touch of her fingertips sent her desire for Bernard through the roof. She wanted to finish the she was having to herself before she stepped in the shower to suck on his freshly washed dick.

Damaris let her fingers dip in and out of her honey pot. She imagined kneeling in the shower before Bernard and grasping his flaccid dick in her hand and sliding it slowly into her barely open mouth while looking up at him. She imagined she would finger herself and suck his dick in the shower.

With erotic memories of their skin touching so fresh in her mind, Damaris saw this thing between them becoming more than a one night or one-time thing. She let her thoughts of desire and contentment from her own hands tell her that she was about to explode with its second orgasm of the morning.

Damaris arched her back, pressing her head into her pillow; she pinched her hardened nipple with one hand. She cupped her breast while her other hand pressed hard against her swollen clit, spreading her legs and letting her fingers slide deep inside herself. She rubbed hard against her clit with the palm of her hand and pushed harder in and out with her fingers. While moaning into the morning sunlight, the sun shone on her face through the sheer curtains in her room. Within seconds, she was shattered with another full-on orgasm. Her fingers soaked, body trembled, and her toes curled up in the sheets.

Hearing the shower turn off, Damaris realized her desire would have to commence without the assistance of a hot shower. She wiped her hands on the sheets and rolled to her side facing the bathroom door.

Bernard stood in the doorway with his hands grasping the doorframe, flexing his entire set of chest and ab muscles while staring at her. She was mesmerized by the 'V'. The white towel barely wrapped around his waist and could easily be removed. His obsidian eyes threw sexual daggers at her. She imagined his bald head between her thighs once again. If she wasn't so sated right now, she would have devoured his body until they both cried from exhaustion. She let her thoughts turn into a wickedly sexy smile. She bit her lower lip and fluttered her eyelashes at him.

She admired every fine inch of his body and he spoke up, "God you're beautiful. You know that, I hope? You are so damn sexy laying there in the morning sunlight. I can't wait until tonight. Hell, I had a hard time waiting these last two weeks to say something."

She thought of how the glow on her face was not from the sunshine, but the last orgasm her fingers gave her pussy as she thought of him. However, she gave him a seductive smile and spoke softly.

"Thank you. I'm excited about tonight. About us."

He took a step forward, nearing the edge of the bed, tilting his head he asked, "Will there be an us? I mean, this doesn't have to end anytime soon. We're great together at work, but that first time our eyes locked; I felt this connection. You know?"

"Yes!" She sat up in bed naked and looked up at him. "I felt it too."

Biting her bottom lip, she let her hand brush his soft dick under his towel. She wanted to suck him, but she was feeling an internal exhaustion to her body from all the sex. She let her hand slide away, rolled off the bed, stood up to stretch and laid a soft kiss on his lips.

"I need to shower." She sauntered off to her bathroom with a wiggle in her ass that taunted him. She heard his appreciative whistle behind her, and it warmed her heart. She was reeling from everything that was happening lately.

For a moment Damaris thought their connection may have never happened considering how shy Bernard seemed to be at the office. It was after that first touch they experienced at the office that she had clear confirmation. She remembered having to ask him a question and headed to his office. His back was to her, and as soon as her hand lay on his shoulder, it seemed a current shot through them; his reaction told her he felt her attraction too. It was all they could do not to kiss each other and tear each other's clothes off in his office. Instead, she handed him the report and told him the first drink was on her that night.

The water from the shower couldn't wash away the permanent smile on her face. She slowly lathered her breasts and sensitive pussy with a coconut body wash and thought of all the things she wanted to happen between them. Most of all, she wanted to wake up Sunday morning at his place doing exactly what they did at hers.

Stepping out of the bathroom, she had on a blue silk robe, her hair was wrapped in a towel and a smile still creased on her face. He was dressed in his work clothes from the previous day. He wrapped his hands around her face and pulled her in for a gentle kiss. When he pulled back, he looked a little sad.

"I don't want to go, but then I don't think you should have to kick me out either. I'm sure you have plans for today. I'll be leaving here a happy man as long as I know we're still on for tonight?"

"Yes!" She exclaimed smiling at him coyly.

Bernard exhaled deeply, "Great! Well, I live like a bachelor, and my place can use a little sprucing up before you come over tonight, but I want to cook you dinner. Italian, ok?" He questioned.

"Yes. Italian would be great. Can I bring the wine?" She asked rubbing her hands up and down his back and looking into his dark eyes.

"If you want. I mean I can stop at the liquor store on the way and have it chilled by the time you make it. Unless you want to just bring something, sure, you can get that. Oh yeah, pack an overnight bag."

Inside she felt good about how fast things were taking off. She took a step closer and laid her hands on his chest. "Go do whatever it is you think you need to do, but I'm already impressed. Add the fact you cook, well that makes you even sexier. See you at six?"

"Well, I wanted you at four, but if you need the time…"

"I do, and Bernard, something tells me you might too. Relax, last night was fantastic. Tonight, let's just relax, have fun and let the chips fall where they may. Just the fact that we've finally gotten together is a relief to my senses. Looking at you every day and wondering... well let's just say you've surpassed my imagination." She smiled at his puffed chest and proud look. *He should be proud because between her legs, his tongue was like magic, his fingers were exquisite and his Johnson, well size does matter,* she joked internally.

"Go, I've got girlie things to do." She pushed him towards the door. She laughed as he turned with a smitten smile on his face. He turned back and kissed her one more time and made his exit.

At six o'clock on the dot, Damaris rang Bernard's doorbell from the outside secure door. She left her wrap pinned up with decorative pins, her large purse was packed with a few overnight essentials and an extra cute little sundress rolled up and tucked neatly inside. Her three-inch wedge sandals were a tan versatile, and her soft pink sheer dress had only a pink slip-dress under it with small straps. No bra or no panties were worn. Why bother, they were coming off before first course anyway, she was sure of it. Damaris' fingernails and toenails were painted a soft pink; she wore a silver toe ring that interconnected with a silver ankle bracelet, and small diamond earrings. Her perfume gave her a sultry feeling that great things were going to happen.

She spent the entire day remembering the way Friday played out; from his reaction to her first touch to him ending up in her bed. Damaris recollected on the flash of fire in his eyes and the rise in his pants. Drinks at the bar had them laughing and relaxing in no time, but the shared cab ride and their erotic kisses could only have ended up as if it did.

Now here she stood, being buzzed in to his place. Every good girl notion of taking it too fast, being too forward went with the light summer breeze outside. Sometimes a girl just has to take that first step and play it out with hopes it ends romantically.

She watched him open the door with a beautiful bouquet of salmon-colored roses mixed with baby's breath. She exchanged the bottle of red wine for the roses and held them up to her nose to breathe their fragrant scent.

"Thank you, they're lovely." She kissed him softly on the lips.

"Welcome." He spoke nervously as he stepped aside, and she took her first steps in.

It was a corner apartment with lots of earth tones and homely feel. The quintessential bachelor pad. Bernard's place was nice, but she wasn't there to judge his place. She wanted his shaft inside her, his mouth between her legs and another rocking night of spectacular sex. However, the soft music playing, the crackling fireplace under the obscenely large TV, the lit candles on the table set for two was a nice romantic touch that made her smile.

"I have a vase for those flowers on the counter. I just wanted to present them to you; hopefully you won't be taking them home until morning." Bernard stated his eyebrows raised slightly.

She toyed with him. "If tonight will be anything like last night, I plan on waking to the sun in your room this time." She reached up and kissed him lightly. When she pulled away to put the flowers in the vase of water, he seemed relieved.

"Well, the lasagna is about a half-hour away from being done. Shall we start with a glass of wine and appetizers?"

"Yes."

Walking over to his kitchen next to where he was looking for a bottle opener, she saw two wine glasses on the counter. She realized that he put a lot into making the night special. That meant a lot to her.

This was not to be just another night of sex, there were officially on a date and that made her body ignite with passionate desire.

"Bernard?" She whispered.

"Yes?" He turned and looked at her with a sexual hunger that she understood so well.

"I can be the appetizer." She lifted her slip and dress over her head revealing her stark nakedness. "I need you now."

She didn't have to ask twice. The hunger in his eyes ignited as he wrapped her up in his arms for a possessive hungry kiss. When he pulled away, he guided her to his leather couch. There was already a soft blanket laid out on part of the couch, and she smiled. He had plans.

She let her hands wander to his dress shirt and unbuttoned one button at a time while looking into his eyes. "You have a nice place, but I'm not here for the design."

"Thanks." A light chuckle came out of his mouth. His hands were already caressing her skin with soft gentle grazes over her body.

As soon as she got his shirt off, she ran her hands over his cuts reveling in what was coming. She looked into his eyes with a smiling, "I came here for this." Letting her hand graze over the solid print in his pants, "And mostly this."

He surprised her as he spoke rapidly. "I want this." He laid her back before she even had his pants undone. He gently spread her legs and let his hands stroke the inside of her thighs as his eyes looked at her with passion. "You want this? You like this? You get all crazy when I lick your pussy."

"Yes!" The excitement in her own tone exited her mouth without thought.

She let one hand rest to the side of his head gently while he separated her sweet bald pussy lips with his fingers. He licked her and looked at her moan. She stroked his hair with her fingers while her other hand gently squeezed and played with her nipple. It was hard and sensitive, so she let the palm of her hand brush it gently across causing a quick quivering to her senses.

His tongue licked her with quick lashes; she felt his fingers dip inside to her wet pussy. She ached for his joystick. She wanted his mouth to suck her to the brink and then for him to enter his thick hardness into her pussy. She moaned out several repetitive words to let him know her pleasure. "Yes! Like that! Oh, yes! That feels so good. I want it daddy. Suck my pussy!"

She wanted him, all of him. She felt the intensity build as he massaged her bald pussy with his fingers. He licked and sucked on her clit while his fingers slid in and out of her slick pussy like an orchestrated event. In and out. In and out.

"Ah..." The sound escaped her lips as her senses heightened.

The exquisite way he dipped his fingers in her tight, wet pussy. His lashes on her swollen clit had her wanting to release her orgasm.

She felt his name on the tip of her tongue, and she wanted to scream out her pleas insisting that her take her. Her body convulsed, and her juiced surrounded his fingers. She felt the repetitive vibration of her pussy clinching and her body tingled. Her eyes closed shut hard and fast. She felt her hands go to his head and push him back, letting long stream gush everywhere. One long word rang out with excitement. "Yes!"

She did what she wanted to do since the foreplay started, she screamed out his name for all to hear. "Oh, Bernard!"

As soon as she felt some type of ability to release him from her clutches, she felt his strength as he gathered her up in his arms and held her. His kisses started at the top of her head. His caring nature in the way he stroked her hair and practically sang into her ear, gripped her heart. "Damaris! I'm right here. Ride it out baby. You're so beautiful when you cum."

During her orgasmic haze, she wanted his dick in her mouth. She sat up and kissed him lightly on the lips. He stood up, and she reached for his hand. "Take your pants off, I want to taste you." She sat up on her knees, pushed her breasts together, and looked up at him seductively. "Let me suck your dick until you want me to turn around and fuck me like I know you like. You like my ass in the air at you don't you."

"God yes!" Struggling with his pants, he trembled. When he was finally out of them, she positioned herself at the perfect height and flicked her tongue across the head. She had her hand wrapped around his dick and sliding it into her mouth with a sucking motion that instantly caused him to moan towards the ceiling in pleasure. His hand was tangled in her hair and he moaned out.

"Yeah, like that. Suck me like that. You're so beautiful. Yeah, that feels so good."

She let her hand stroke between her mouth sucking and licking the tip of his dick. She could feel his desire to cum as the grip of her hair was tighter. She could tell he wanted to shove himself into her mouth, deeply. Instead, he pulled away and practically growled out a command. "Put that ass up for me, Baby. I need to fuck that sweet pussy of yours."

Bernard was in control now. His demands told her he wanted to be in charge. She turned herself around. She propped herself up so she could rest her hands on the back of the couch and spread her legs. She pushed her ass back towards him. He gave her ass a light smack and growled. "God, you have such a great ass!" Then without another word, he slid slowly into her tight pussy.

Her hand left the couch and dipped between her legs to relieve the pressure on her clit that was aching for a touch. She felt his thrusts get harder as he pushed in and out. She rubbed her clit as his hands caressed her hips, guiding them back and forth.

Their moans were singing in the air over the soft music playing in the background. The slapping of skin between them, and the way her fingers felt rubbing herself. It only took a moment; she shattered with him inside pulsing against his dick with an orgasm. She pushed her ass back hard against him as her body shook. She felt him tense and release his cum in the condom inside her.

Just as their breathing was trying to regain some normalcy, the buzzer for the dinner went off. They both started to laugh, and then she finally felt him pull away.

"I'm going to freshen up." She sauntered by him bending over naked in the kitchen to pull the lasagna out. On her way by, she picked up her dress and heels and walked away with a big smile on her face.

The rest of the night was not about his great cooking or the perfect bottle of wine she had chosen. It was about them talking briefly about the aftermath the both of them had and how they wanted to make this a permanent thing. He had asked if he could announce it at the office, and she smiled. "Only if you do that first thing you did to me one more time before I leave tomorrow, and I think you could convince me." Her smile was wicked and devious, but his reaction was that of a challenge accepted. When faced with a desire and a challenge, would your response be?

# Touchdown

Kashauna raced home, pushing her little Red Corolla to its limits and blowing at least two stop signs. It was Sunday night and she planned to teach her husband a lesson by breaking him of his obsessive fantasy sports fetish. She didn't mind his football so much; it was the neglect she faced when the season started. Torrence ate, slept and drank football. She had needs, she only wanted a little affection. During football season, she was lucky to get a peck on the cheek. Kass skidded to a stop in the driveway and ran in the house throwing her purse somewhere near the table by the front door. Convinced she had at least a few minutes to spare, she raced through the bedroom and changed into her sexiest exercise outfit, her Atlanta Falcons fitted tee that was two sizes too small and her black and red trimmed boy shorts before running back to the table at the front door to gather

her purse. She took it to the living room where her husband kept his laptop.

Kashauna inserted the flash drive and downloaded the contents to her husband's computer. Her eyes flashed continuously at the front door. She dug another flash drive out of her purse and replaced the first one in the computer. She was surprised she could even get into his computer. With all the bitching and threatening she did the last two seasons, she was sure he would have put a password on it to keep her from messing with his Fantasy Football stuff. Worried that Torrence might come through the door any second, Kashauna quickly loaded the contents of the flash drive onto the computer. When she was done she shut down the computer and placed it as best as she could in the exact position as she found it.

Kashauna was already on her exercise bike when Torrence opened the door and made a beeline to his laptop. Plopping down in his favorite recliner in the living room, he greeted his wife.

"How was your day?" Torrence said obviously feigning interest since he was already opening his laptop.

"You doing that fantasy football crap again?" Kashauna said as she pedaled a little faster. She felt she had to complain just enough so he would not catch on to her little ruse.

"It's Tuesday night, you know I always get updated league stats on Tuesday." Torrence said.

"Whatever," Kashauna shouted over the whirring of her exercise bike, pretending like she was pissed about his usual inattention.

She wasn't really pissed. She knew soon her plan was going to be set in motion, and she would have her husband's full attention. She pedaled even faster as she glanced over at him, waiting for his computer to start up.

"What the…" Torrence said when his computer started up and the video began to play.

Kashauna ignored him, hoping he would continue to watch. She slowed her pedaling and Torrence watched the video of her exercising in the nude on his computer. Her friend from work gave her a simple program on a flash drive that started the video, but wouldn't let it stop until it was finished. As long as Torrence didn't get up and walk away, he would be watching her dance to a Zumba exercise program for the next twenty minutes.

Kass felt her mouth stretch into a smile as her husband sank into his chair continuing to watch the video instead of complaining about it. Convinced he was not too far gone in his addiction to his fantasy league, she stopped pedaling and climbed off the bike. It appeared her plan was beginning to work and with any luck she would break her husband's fantasy football addiction and make sure she became his fantasy again.

She padded quietly to her husband, stood behind him, and watched the image of herself naked, dancing and exercising in her bedroom. Torrence didn't even look up from the computer. He seemed perfectly happy watching her image dance in front of him while the real person stood silent behind him. Kashauna felt a bead of sweat roll down her bare back and into the crack of her ass.

She was still hot from pedaling and her heart was still pounding in her chest, but not just from the exercise. She looked at Torrence's lap and saw a bulge forming in the crotch of his pants tenting the dark fabric of his slacks. She knew it would be on and popping and she was not planning to stop until she had her fill.

"You like what you see?" Kashauna asked running her hands inside Torrence's shirt over the hairs on his chest.

"Oh yeah, I like it, when did you make this?" He said.

"Don't worry about it," She responded. "Just enjoy the show!" She moved her hands down across his belt and onto the stretched fabric over his crotch.

Kass felt Torrence's hardness through his pants straining for release against the fabric of his pants. A twinge of excitement flashed over her at the thought of him working that thing around her outer lips and across her clit. She thought about him pushing into her slow and steady, stretching and filling her. She wanted to pull it out and feel it in her hands, stroke his length, but she knew, if her plan was going to work she had to wait. Instead, she glided her hands back up Torrence's shirt and began unbuttoning it from the top, one button at a time.

Kashauna pulled Torrence's shirt open and exposed his beautifully formed chest, and the ripples of tight muscle on his abdomen. Looking up at her, he reached for her trying to meet his lips with hers.

"Watch the movie," she commanded guiding his head back toward the computer screen.

Coercing him back to the video was hard. She wanted desperately to feel his kiss, feel his stubble tickling and scratching her skin as he probed her mouth with his tongue, but she had to deny herself for now. She had to be in control and bring him to the brink; otherwise she wouldn't be able to manipulate him the way she wanted. Once he was facing the computer, she let her hands travel across his chest and slowly down the sexy bumps of his stomach and around the waistband of his pants.

Kashauna slid her fingers down until she was able to wriggle them under the waistband of his boxers and onto the soft curls at the base of his dick. He let out a little groan as she ran both hands over the length of him and back to the base. That was all she needed to hear, and she knew that from that point on she was going to be in control, at least as long as she could stand it. She felt her own juices build as she touched him. Kashauna rotated her hips in a dancing motion and her outer folds became slick and warm. She wanted him, bad, and she could just strip and let him take her on the spot, but she wanted to make him wait. Kashauna wanted to make Torrence work as hard as she had to make this extraordinary.

The computer showed her doing lunges. Her body already started to glisten with sweat and her boobs bounced when she jogged in place. She nearly laughed out loud at the merriment of seeing herself on the video naked as the day she was born with her boobs bouncing up and down. The video certainly excited Torrence, and that made her exultant.

Kashauna brushed Torrence's hand away at least three times while she slowly worked his belt loose. She unfastened his pants and worked the zipper until his stiffness pushed through the opening barely restrained by his boxers. She rolled his chair back just enough to kneel in front of him. Kashauna pulled his trousers down, as he slipped his shoes off and tore at his shirt until it lay in a pile of shredded fabric on the floor. He moaned again as she knelt down between his legs. His manhood, strained against the thin fabric of his boxer shorts, a tiny dark wet spot formed on the fabric. Kashauna looked up at Torrence and grabbed his boxers at the fly and pulled until the button popped. The fabric ripped from top to bottom and his stiff dick sprang forth and stood at attention. He looked down at her prying his eyes from the video and licked his lips. Kass reached beside the chair pulled out the warm wet towel she had sitting in the warming bowl. She wrapped the towel around his dick pulling up and down slowly making sure to clean the creases around the head. Kass picked up her frozen bottle of water and took a small sip. She planned to work every last drop as she took him in both her hands stroking from base to tip and back.

"Don't look at me, watch the video. If you look down at me again, I'll stop. You understand?" Kashauna said.

"Yes, I understand." Torrence said turning his focus back on the computer.

Kashauna smiled to herself while Torrence turned his attention to the laptop. She kept looking up at him waiting for him to break his concentration. She leaned in close enough to allow her hot breath to blow across his dick. It jumped in her hands and Torrence moaned again. She stuck out her tongue and licked the underside of it from the base to the tip. She tasted his salty pre-cum on her tongue and she rolled it over and around his tip, then she took him fully into her mouth.

As soon as she closed her lips around his pole and rolled her tongue around the tip, she felt his hands on her shoulders. She looked up and saw him looking down at her with a grimacing look of serious concentration on his face. She stopped, pulled herself away from him, reached up, and brushed his hands off her shoulders.

"I said, watch the video, or I stop," she demanded trying to sound as mean and forceful as she could despite her own need to feel his touch.

Torrence snapped his head back up and looked at the laptop. He brought his hands to rest gripping the chair, holding his hands together to keep from reaching out for her again. Once he did as he was told, Kass took him into her mouth again working her lips down over the bulbous head of his dick swirling her tongue around it as she stroked it with both of her hands.

She loved the feel of his wood in her mouth. She enjoyed the control she had, it gave her dominant satisfaction. She never really enjoyed giving head much before him, and now she achieved a kind of pleasure from pleasuring him. She always enjoyed receiving oral sex more than giving it, but his reaction to her excited her in some strange way. Beyond the pleasure of his reaction, she felt a sense of control over him when giving him head. She assumed he felt the same way when he went down on her. It was all about control.

Torrence moaned again and to moved his hips forward and backward on the chair. Kass took him into her mouth as far as she could. Cupping his balls in her hand, she gently kneaded them while moaning and allowing him to feel the vibrations of her voice against his thickness. When the movements of his hips became more urgent, she leaned back bringing him out of her mouth but stroking his length.

"Stay still," she cooed, but not as forceful as the last time.

Kashauna alternated between stroking his tip and sucking it rolling her tongue around his head until she felt his balls tighten in her hands. When she thought he was close but not quite over the edge, she would pull back and simply breath on him until he calmed down enough not to cum on the spot. She heard the music stop on the computer, but kept rolling her tongue over the head, stroking him and kneading his balls tending his "G-spot" until she thought he was on the edge again then she tested his resolve.

"Close your computer," she said wondering if she had his attention enough for him to forget about his stats and concentrated on her instead.

He looked down at her with that wanting, begging, and sad puppy dog look. Kashauna breathed on his dick and kept her mouth an inch away from it. He hesitated trying to move his hips forward and get back in her mouth before finally giving up and slamming the computer lid shut. As soon as snapped the lid closed, Kashauna slowly leaned into him sinking his big dick into her mouth again.

He reached down again, this time pulling at her exercise tee. She backed off him, raised her arms, and let him work the top off her. She felt the cool air over her bare breasts, and her nipples immediately tightened and protruded. Torrence leaned back, looked at her breasts, licked his lips, and shook his head.

"Damn, I love your tits," he growled as he cupped his hands around them squeezing them inward until she felt the pressure on her sensitive nipples.

Kashauna considered her breasts one of her best assets. Even though she worked out all the time, she didn't lose much in size, and she knew Torrence especially liked the way her nipples popped out like turkey timers at the slightest stimulation. She felt a smile creeping across her face when she saw the way he looked at them. She felt a little giggle working up as she remembered him saying her nipples were like little chocolate drops on a pillow. The comment was always followed with him telling her everything was great with chocolate, and then he would let out an evil little laugh.

Torrence dove into her, licking one breast then the other, rolling his tongue around each nipple sending sparks through her body in a direct path to her core.

*Now it's time for me to get mine*, she thought as she ran her fingers through the hairs on his chest. Although it started out with her controlling him long enough for him to not have time to devote to his fantasy league. Above that, she wanted him to be happy and she figured the best way to do that was to let him pleasure her while keeping him on edge until she was ready.

Kashauna leaned her head back and ran her hands down Torrence's back scratching upward along his spine and across his shoulders as she moved her hands back up his back. Torrence moaned against her scratching, grabbing her breasts hard and craning his neck to kiss her. As soon as their lips met, Torrence placed his hands on the back of her head pushing her into him harder. His aggression pleased her. As he pushed his lips to hers, she wondered if he could taste himself on her. The thought of it turned her on even more.

As soon as she felt his lips part against hers, she darted her tongue into his mouth probing deep and desperate letting him know how excited he was making her. He responded by bringing his hands back to her breasts, making her sigh into his mouth as he brushed his thumbs across her rigid nipples. She brought her hands down his back, over his ass, around his thighs and across his groin until she gripped his stiff dick in both hands. She stroked him gently and he moved in rhythm against her hands. She leaned forward placing her breast around the shaft of his manhood while her lips claimed the tip.

Ten minutes later, she reluctantly broke the kiss, and stood. He pulled down her exercise shorts without a word as she stood. He pulled her shorts to her feet and she quickly kicked them off. Seeing he was eye-level with her bare pussy, she moved a leg up placing her foot on the chair under his leg. Grabbing the back of his head, she pushed him into her.

"Lick it," She said roughly.

He grunted, and she grabbed the back of his bald head, pushing him in even further.

"Eat my pussy," Kass moaned gruffly.

She felt a little self-conscious as soon as she said it, but he obeyed. Kashauna knew did the right thing when she felt his tongue sweep across her moist folds and over her clit. She leaned back against the table at some extreme angle propping herself up with one hand while squeezing her breast and nipple with the other. She felt Torrence's fingers moving around her folds spreading her outer lips. He dove into her with his tongue forging a slippery trail upwards over her inner folds before reaching the summit and circling her clit.

The sudden sensation of his lips closing around her engorged clit, and sucking it into his mouth, sent a shiver through her body so strong she nearly shook him off her.

"Oh Baby, that's it. Suck it," left her mouth before she could think of something more pleasant to say.

Under the circumstances, her outburst fueled him on and he moaned some indecipherable words into her pussy sending another shiver through her body, making her toes curl. Torrence slipped two fingers into Kashauna moving them in slow circles and she nearly collapsed into Torrence's face. He found her cum button, and she was skyrocketing quickly to orgasm. She felt a kind of pressure, a rumbling, like distant thunder, that told her she was on the apex, and quite possibly about the experience the best orgasm ever.

His tongue swept across her clit again as he fervently pumped his fingers into her, she moaned.

"Fuckin' yes. Right there," she yelled through gritted teeth.

What followed was a series of moans and swear words that she thought must have come from someone else's mouth other than hers. Her entire body shook, forcing her to grab hold of his head and pull him deeper into her against her fear of suffocating him. Her orgasm shot through her body in waves lapping at every nerve ending like the flames from a bonfire lapping at the sky.

She felt her body give way and lose control. She started to fall, losing her slippery grip of the table edge. Torrence withdrew his fingers and tongue leaving her desperate and wanting in the midst of her orgasm. Reaching behind her ass, he picked her up. He moved her until her breasts were level with his face. He licked at her breast and nuzzled his face in her ample cleavage and picked her up and lay her on the table on top of his laptop. Over the pounding in her ears, and the lightning coursing through her body, she heard a crack as her ass came in contact with the table and laptop.

"Your computer," she said as she felt the warmth of his laptop on her ass cheeks.

"I don't give a shit," Torrence said lifting her and sweeping the computer off the table and into the wall.

She heard the computer crash against the wall on the far side of the room, but had no time to speak. Torrence was spreading her legs, and her body hummed in anticipation. She felt his hand on her breast again gently squeezing it and sliding his slippery fingers upward until he pinched her nipple between his thumb and forefinger. At the same time, she felt the head of his thickness gliding along her slit teasing, searching, until it passed across her sensitive clit making her cry out in ecstasy.

The feeling of his dick on her clit was so intense it was almost painful, but she craved more.

She felt her pussy contracting again as another wave washed over her. She was not sure whether she was having another orgasm, or if she was still in her last one. All the sensations seemed to fuse together. Then, he slowly slid into her. The fullness of his girth stretched her as he pushed himself into her slow and steady at first, she screamed out some kind of swear word even she couldn't understand.

Torrence moved into Kass until she felt his curly dick hairs brushing against her over-sensitive clit before moving back and letting his head tickle her folds. Her entire body was on fire. Her pussy repeatedly contracted and grabbed at his dick. He pushed its full length slowly back into her. Her body was floating on a cloud miles above the earth and he pushed into her with rhythm and fervency. For what seemed an eternity, she sang with him in a vivid symphony of curse words and angry demands.

She held on to him ripping at his body until she feared she would tear his flesh from him. Kass yelled at him to push harder, go deeper, not to stop. He let out a series of long low moans and thrust himself into her until he pushed her entire body across the table. He twisted her sensitive nipples so hard, she screamed out, and he collapsed onto her lapping at her sore nipples. They held their position, afraid to move and send another assault of intensity to their raw and sensitive nerves.

When they both recovered enough to move again, Kashauna went to the bathroom to shower. After the water started running hot, Torrence joined her. He lovingly washed her body, too spent to even form a substantial erection as he washed her breasts, and between her legs. He hurriedly washed himself, and left the shower before her. After she dried her body and combed out her hair she wrapped a towel around herself and strolled out of the bathroom. Stopping by their bedroom, she pulled the neatly wrapped package from under the bed.

Walking into the living room, Kass saw Torrence standing over his broken laptop and suddenly felt bad for him.

"I'm sorry about your laptop," she said and actually meant it.

Torrence looked at her and a wry smile spread slowly across his face.

"I'm alright. If you continue to treat me like that I can reschedule some things." He said.

Smiling, she mouthed "thank you." Bringing the box around to the front of her she asked, "Would you like to open the box or the towel?"

Torrence kicked his broken computer to the side, licked his lips, and took the present and placed it on his recliner, and flicked her towel to the floor.

*Mission accomplished,* she thought to herself as he wrapped his arms around her and planted a sloppy kiss on her mouth. His tongue eagerly probed for hers

and sent electric currents through her body.

Safiya had this dream before, yet each time the dream was more explicit, tantalizing, and erotic. Each time she awoke from her seductive dream, she would relive the memory so fresh on her skin.

Her dream maker provoked her carnal desires. His thick jet black hair professionally trimmed yet it held that sexy bad-boy appeal. His honey-brown eyes sent shivers down her spine. The creamy butter pecan complexion of his skin accented his 5'11" frame. He was a corporate centerfold mixed with bad-boy desire.

This vision of his naked body replayed in her mind. She was filled with provocative thoughts of touching his skin, running her fingers over the waves in his hair, and letting the palms of her hands run over the length of his chest. The thought alone caused a sensation rush over her with the feel of adrenaline.

Last night's dream was about him taking her in a way she sought after. He had shown up at her door ready to seduce her, knowing she was usually off-limits to a man like him. She opened the door dressed in an evening gown with a ducktail that was as sparkly as it was red. It hugged every curve she embraced. When he spoke, the first thing he stated surprised her.

*"I understand you have rules and guidelines. However, I want more. I want to make you scream with hunger, cum in my hands, and tell me that I am worth breaking all those silly rules for."*

In her dream, he states all that so boldly. And as quickly as he enters her modest apartment, her dream maker lays her on the bed fully dressed, but aching for his touch.

Her dream knows what she wants next. She wants him to devour every inch of her skin, lick her pussy with his tongue, and let his pecan stick reside so deep inside that she screams out his name in ecstasy. Her dream maker allows her dream to play this out like an orchestrated symphonic porn movie.

Safiya lay back on her bed, examining how incredibly sexy he looked in his dark business suit and crisp salmon-colored dress shirt. Oh how she would like to be wearing nothing but that dress shirt over her skin as he undressed her.

She felt the strain in his pants so she decided she to be the dominate one. "Take off your clothes." It came out as a sexual demand; one that he followed quickly as his eyes enlarged with a passionate gaze.

She lowered her voice and whispered. "Show me that incredibly sexy body of yours and that full hard dick too. Then undress me with your hands slowly. Kiss me everywhere. Make me crumble into a wet heated mess, and then make me cum all over again."

Mike took her dominating suggestions quite well. His clothes were off and tossed randomly to the corner of her room. He put a hand out and pulled her to him. He kissed her slowly, deeply, while his hands caressed the curves of her body. Then the sound of the zipper on the back of her dress resounded over their breathing as it tickled her skin.

He pulled away from the kiss, turned her around so her back was to him, and lowered her red shiny scrap of material to the ground. Safiya heard the sound of fabric land on the ground around her feet. Her body began to tremble with the delicious thought of what was coming next.

He swept her hair aside and kissed the back of her neck. She heard a whisper in her ear, something about 'so sexy'. She was so far gone, answering was not an option.

His kisses moved from the back of her neck and trailed down her shoulder as the release of her jet-black hair now cascaded down the front of her bare breast on one side. The trail of kisses down her back elicited moans from her lips. This vivid dream was going to the place she wanted. His wet kisses trailed her body and his fingers explored her wetness from behind.

She felt the sensual way his hands were explored her body from behind and the gentle gliding of one of his hand as it caressed her waist. His fingers tickled her skin and lightly explored her body. He worked his way down until he was in position behind her and her imagination ran wild with anticipation.

His lips started at the back of her calves with sweet, gentle, wet kisses moving tenderly up to the inside of the back of her thighs. His hands slowly eased her legs apart, one at a time. A moaning plea left her mouth before she realized he was now the one in control.

A light chuckle of deep manly laughter filled the room as his voice spoke from behind between kisses. "Not tonight. Tonight you're mine, and I'm taking my time. Tonight, I plan to unleash your every sexual desire."

The words coming from his raspy voice sent vibrations to her dripping core. She felt herself tighten and flinch with what could easily have been considered a teaser to the orgasm she was sure would unfold.

Safiya stood statuesque and stark naked; not only in the physical sense, but the mental sense as well. She had always been in charge, both inside and outside the bedroom. However, her dream maker had other plans for her control and desires. Her dream would let Mike Wright take control.

His voice, sultry and methodical took control of her. "You're so wet already." He practically growled with accomplishment as his finger slowly slid from behind.

Safiya wanted to scream, but instead she moaned rhythmically to what he was doing. He was kissing the curve of her ass with his lips and dipping his fingers into her wet folds. His lips moved upward and landed on the small of her back. After romancing her ass, he quickly got to his feet. His hand came around and cupped her breast. His fingers toyed with her nipple as he let his tongue ever so lightly lick the side of her neck. He pulled her into the space of his body letting his naked skin lay against hers. His finger found her swollen clit and brushed it lightly back and forth causing loud encouraging moans to escape her lips.

Safiya was not in control of her dream; it was in control of her. If she were, she would've stuck his throbbing manhood into her tight, wet pussy already. Instead, her dream maker toyed with her sensations causing her to squirm in her sleep under her silky sheets.

His hard dick settled at the top of her ass. His fingers dipped into her wet folds again and again, but not affording her the pleasure of him going in too deep, which she wanted, badly.

A soft whisper against her ear, told her that he was about take control of her body in so many ways. "I'm going to make you cum in my hand, and then I'm going to taste you until you beg me to stop. I'm going to bend you over this bed, putting your sweet, round ass in the air and I'm going to slide into your silky, wet pussy. And then, I'm going to fuck you, like you've never been fucked before."

Mike's voice held promise and intrigue. His fingers dipped inside of her with more intention, not just the soft playing of tender gestures.

She pushed back hard against him wiggling her ass against his hardness, and letting her hands reach back to touch any naked skin she could find.

Her moaning grew so loud that she knew someone could easily speculate what was occurring inside her apartment. Safiya didn't care because this was her moment, one that she intended on finishing with her mental internal orgasm.

His deep growl filled the room and his fingers slid in and out of her letting the palm of his hand brush against her swollen clit. His other hand was holding her breast while his mouth kissed and licked around her neck.

Her body was so sensitive and alive. The orgasm was so close, she was wondering if she could only hold out a moment more to let the dream linger. Safiya was going to cum in his hand with just a few more strokes. She could feel the buildup as he brought her body to a pleasurable euphoria. She released her inhibition, let her legs clamp around his hand, and her body shook with quivering bouts of satiation.

"Oh My God!" She yelled out filling the room with the delightful gasp of joy.

Mike held her close to him for a second. She could feel the throbbing of his dick behind her. His heavy breathing told her what he wanted to do. Mike wanted to fuck her hard and fast. In this dream she wanted that too, yet her dream maker had another plan. She wouldn't feel the pleasure from his hard dick sliding into her wetness just yet. He was going to make her cum again, but this time with his mouth.

With her body still humming and dripping wet, he switched her position on the bed. She felt her arms go up above her head and her legs spread open against the bed. It was so easy for her to look at him and think of what was coming next, he was glorious to look at. His muscles appeared pumped from his exertion; his smile told her he was going to enjoy himself. His eyes lit up and he slowly took in the vision of her immaculate bare pussy.

Mike lowered his face and spread her legs further apart. With the first lash of his tongue, Safiya moaned with intense pleasure. His tongue was strong, mouth hot, and smooth. He had a way of doing things to her down there. She moved her hands from above her head and slammed them down on the bed and she held on for dear life.

Her heavy breathing and moaning only invigorated him. He knew she was close, so very close. With her heavy moans and pleas, her wiggling, it hit her so fast. He latched on and sucked as hard as she shivered; sending quick electric pulses her body.

Moments later, a whisper of air passed down there. She opened her eyes in time to see him triumphantly slide his hard, sheathed dick inside of her warmth. With eyes darkened and wide, his chest puffed, and his muscular body started to position itself over her body. She watched the pleasure she gave him as he slid into her slowly. Safiya was tight from her orgasms and still pulsing with pleasure. He slowly slid in a few inches at a time and moaned. Her hands went up to his arms and stroked his muscles. She looked into his eyes while still slowly sliding in and out loosening her for his width. She wrapped her legs around his back and lifted her hips so he could glide against her swollen clit and lead her to her third orgasm of the night.

Just as Safiya came in her dream with him pulsing and tensing, she awoke with a smile on her face. Safiya wanted her dream to really happen, yet as of late he was still as unobtainable as the first day she saw him. She wanted all that to change. Getting out of bed and made her way to the kitchen, she formulated a plan.

Night fell and her loft was pitch-black. Safiya watched him from across the way as she often did. She patiently waited for him to come home and follow his nightly routine. Directly across the street from his, her condo provided the perfect view. Coincidence or fate could be to blame, yet something told her what she was going to do in the coming days was wickedly sinful.

That 'he' she watched patiently on nights like this, was one Michael Wright. A successful businessman in the area and their only interaction was an occasional run-in at the local market and brief social interaction. Although he didn't know who she was, her picture and name were figments of her vivid imagination.

She made it her dirty little secret. The timing of her trips to the market. The silent cautious watching. Her friends would think she were crazy if they knew about the man. It wasn't that she couldn't have any man she wanted. She could. She just couldn't stop wanting this one particular man.

In the nighttime reflection of her bay window, she caught an image of herself with her piercing black eyes and jet-black hair. She wore it just past her shoulder blades in a straight cut. Tonight she wore a blue silk robe with no panties or bra. She couldn't wait to see Mike's nightly routine.

She wondered if he knew how incredibly sexy he was, especially when he worked out in the spare room directly across from her living room. The room she was taking up residence in sitting in her overstuffed dark chocolate leather chair, facing his direction.

This nightly routine often ended with her masturbating to a complete bone shattering orgasm and a good night's sleep. Safiya needed that sleep, she craved it. She wouldn't be able to endorse her clients successfully without it.

The complication in this whole scenario wasn't what Michael Wright was, but who he was.

Seducing her building's landlord wasn't exactly how a successful business woman behaved. However, she couldn't help it. Running into him had been chance just like him living across the way. That was fate.

Mike's Real Estate Company had him owning pads all over town. He was successfully taking advantage of the market. Like clockwork, when he was in town he came home at seven o'clock. He would start out with a protein shake, check his computer, make a call, and workout. The workout was her favorite part. He would shower and then strut around his place in only a towel. Usually, he went out or had a flavor of the week stop by and then leave as soon as the deed was done. On more than a rare occasion, she would watch him sit and read a book. He seemed to favor the Bestselling Author K'wan.

It was the workout part that got Safiya worked up. She would achieve that first orgasm then. She would take a moment to collect herself, maybe have a nice glass of wine, she would freshen up and then inevitably with the vision of him strutting around in a towel she would have a second one.

Thinking of him, she brushed her silk robe aside and rubbed her nipple to tautness. The feel of the raw silk on her skin was divine. The slickness of the warming massage oil she dabbed on her fingers felt even better while she toyed with her nipple. She let her hand wander from breast to breast, each nipple grew rigid. She let the palm of her hand brush across the nipple creating a tingling sensation on each breast.

She knew how to make herself feel good. It was survival of the fittest, and she didn't go sleeping around with men just for the hell of it. She had one standby for a quick fix, strictly sex, but lately all she could do was think of Mike and her self-satisfying moments in front of the window watching him.

The light of Mike's apartment flipped on and the show started. She watched his routine start out like clockwork. This time, instead of a business suit, he had on a pair of faded Areopostale jeans that fit nice in the places she imagined touching, gripping, licking and sucking until he came in her mouth.

Safiya watched him grab the hem of his tee shirt and take it off exposing the nice set of chest muscles and abs she adored. She wanted to run her fingertips over that chest and massage it. She fantasized about licking the sweat from his body after his workout and letting her hand take that sweat and wrap it around his dick with a firm grip.

Mike paced back in forth, in his bare feet and only those jeans. She wished he would take the jeans off and pace. She let her hand wander across her belly and rub between her legs on her inner thigh. She was warming up her intentions just watching him pace back and forth. He seemed upset about something, but that didn't stop her from wanting him, and it didn't stop her from pleasuring herself either.

His phone rang and he went to it quickly. She watched him run his hand over those thick waves and hold it there as if he was agitated. After a few moments tense moments from him, he threw the phone across the room. He kept pacing. She desperately wanted to pleasure him and help him work whatever was going on out.

Safiya let two fingers dip deep inside of herself to bring the moisture to her clit. While her other hand pinched her nipple again. The slickness she accumulated from thinking of him was amusing. Tonight her clit seemed ultra-sensitive. She was going for four orgasms. Soon they would meet face to face for the very first time and she needed to work him out of her system.

Just as the palm of her hand brushed over her sensitive clit, she felt the first of a quick convulsion. She stopped and focused on Mike who was now facing her directly. His hands were up against the floor to ceiling glass window. His gaze was down on the street. Then his gaze slowly lifted and looked directly at her. Safiya knew he couldn't possibly see her through her darkened window. With her lights off no one could see in, yet it felt as if he was directing his stare at her.

With his intense stare in her direction, she proceeded to make herself feel good. She didn't need to watch him workout to cum. With him standing there facing her with his bare chest and jeans that made him look like a sex god, she would cum with just that.

Her hand grasped and released her breast; she pinched her nipple and brushed her palm across. With her other hand, she took one finger, then two and pushed them deep inside her wetness. She let the palm of her hand press down on her swollen clitoris while she pushed in and out. Safiya looked at him like he could see the sexual exhibition she was putting on for him. She wondered if he would love to watch in person.

With her legs propped up and her head tilted sideways, she arched her back and found her pleasure. Her clit felt so ultra-sensitive. The pressure caused her to cum so hard. Her walls pulsated and tightened around her fingers. Her palm sent another shockwave through her body with a slight movement. Her toes curled into the cushion of the leather chair.

The feeling of something traveling through her body caused her to moan sensually. Her hand on her breast traveled from one to the next grasping at it. She collapsed with her fingers still inside of her dripping wet pussy and her hand pressed hard against her clitoris. A slow lingering laughter built up within her. She afforded herself the pleasure of the laughter.

Mike was that desirable and without touching her could make her cum. She was so fulfilled, that if she only did this once tonight, she would be sated. She caught his look of inquisitiveness. It was as if he had seen it all. The show she put on in private. Shaking his head, he pushed away from the window and walked towards his kitchen. Safiya, on the other hand, needed to freshen up and get a glass of wine for round two.

Tomorrow was going to be a busy day of meetings and introductions. Her introducing the owner of the company, Michael Wright, to her entire team of graphic designers, display builders and office staff of Safiya Graphics, Inc. She was a bit nervous, but she knew her job and she did it well. She hired great staff and their designs were well known.

The only thing she wasn't confident in was the private meeting her and Mr. Michael Wright would have. Could she keep her hands to herself or would she want to take him right there in the private confines of her office? More than likely it would be the latter of the two.

She walked into her kitchen of stainless steel appliances and granite countertops. She wanted Mike to eat her pussy spread eagle on her countertop like a buffet. She giggled to herself lightly at the fantasies she was creating. However, with Mike, she thought it might be possible.

Safiya poured herself a full glass of wine. She took a deep sip and let the feel of the dark-red wine settle on her palate. Her wine choice had a bit of sweetness instead of the typical bitterness. She let the wine settle until it was warm in her mouth, then she swallowed imaging how Mike would taste when she swallowed his sweet seed.

The moonlight from outside positioned just right, allowed her to navigate about her apartment with grace. She could only see the outlines of her furniture. She moved from her kitchen back to the windows that ran the length of Mike's apartment. She wondered if he ever thought someone might be watching him. Anyone who has ever lived in a condo knew you were like a peep show unless your windows were tinted.

The light in Mike's workout room flipped on. He was out of those sexy jeans and in his typical attire of Nike gym shorts and tee shirt. She went to the windowpane that was directly across from his workout room. Safiya loosened the tie on her robe letting it fall open. She placed one hand on the cool glass of the window.

With an imaginary toast towards Mike, she spoke to herself. "To my dream maker. May the orgasm be intense!" Safiya took a sip of her wine and set it on the ledge of the window.

He seemed to be working out with more than usual intensity. She wondered what frustrations he had to work out. She desired to be the one to pleasure him until the stress was gone, but pleasuring herself would do.

Safiya let her hand slide up her body to her breast. She toyed with her nipple until it was taut. Letting the feel of her pinching and brushing motion torment her senses, she let the hand that was on the window tease her other nipple. She played back and forth, grabbing and squeezing her breasts to pinching her nipples, to brushing the palms of her hands over the taunt nipples. It felt so good, so right while she watched Mike.

She let her robe slide off her naked body, her hands brought pleasure to her breasts and slowly slid down between her legs again.

The sill of the tall windows was the right height for her to set her naked foot on the ledge. She let one of her hands slide up her body to her neck. Rubbing her neck with one hand, the other hand eased between her legs, brushing her palm across her naked pussy. The moisture accumulated.

Her fingers toyed with her pussy and Mike stepped his game up. He practically tore his tee shirt off, wiped the sweat from his head of full dark-brown hair, and tossed it aside. He did chin-ups on a bar and the sweat glistened on his skin. The flexing of his muscles and her yearning to fuck him caused a slow wave of yearning to build to intensity.

Safiya imagined his hands on her body. She let her fingers pull slickness from within and moisten her clit some more. She could sense her orgasm coming. She focused on his naked body, his muscles flexing, and his sweat dripping. She dipped two fingers inside and thrust quickly. By the third thrust, she had three fingers in and her palm pressed hard against her swollen clit. She pulsed to the beat of Mike pulling up and releasing on the pull-up bar.

With a pinch of her nipple and a deep hard thrust of her fingers she came. Cum surrounded her fingers, the walls of her vagina tightened and her clit convulsed with the wave of the orgasm. She continued to apply pressure to her clit, tilted her head back, and moaned with pleasure.

When her head rolled forward and her fingers pulled out, Mike was standing against the glass window again, looking in her direction. Looking as if he saw her cum. Watching as if he needed to see her, talk to her, or better yet, fuck her.

The next morning Safiya thought back to when she first accepted this offer. She knew her marketing skills could send Michael Wright's Real estate Company to the next level. Her last contracted job was doing exceptionally well and this one would too. She just needed to maintain her composure while in his presence.

∞∞∞∞∞∞∞∞

Mike was due in at any minute, and her nerves were still on edge. She had to pull it together. She stared at herself in the bathroom mirror. Her jet-black hair was styled straight today with a touch of gloss that it had dark red shimmers in just the right light. Those red shimmers played off her sienna skin.

Safiya looked like a dominatrix; she wore an all-black, tight-fitting suit, knee-high black leather boots that sat against her calves like a second skin. She wore a red shirt beneath her suit jacket; she stared at herself satisfied she looked classy instead of trashy.

Safiya took a deep, cleansing breath. She ran her sweaty hands under cold water for a second and lit the cool tingle through her veins. She dried her hands and slipped a second coat of MAC Ruby Woo on her lips. Blowing the mirror a kiss, she strutted out the door like the Boss she was. *Ready or not, here I come,* she thought to herself.

There was some commotion coming from one of the rooms down the hall, it dawned on her that the meeting was about to start. Mike was in the office and everyone was bustling about trying to look busy. Her team worked incredibly hard under pressure, but anytime you had to meet the boss for the first time, nerves unraveled.

Safiya fully expected an entourage to be with Mike, a limo driver, a secretary, or an aid, but it was just him. Sitting outside at the rear of the lot, was a jet-black Chevy Impala. After parking his car, Mike exited dressed in a black suit and red-striped tie. He walked casually towards the entrance, straightening his tie and carrying a black leather briefcase. His confident stride screamed sexy, at least to Safiya it did. There wasn't anything the man couldn't do that wasn't sexy in her mind.

Safiya casually walked to the reception area as the hustle of all the employees faded out. The receptionist applied fresh make-up and was flinging her burnt red locs as Safiya walked by. However, Safiya knew his type. He liked thick, tall, dark-haired women, similar to herself. She saw them many times at his place.

Mike walked through the front door and Safiya put on her wickedly sexy smile and stood with confidence. Mike, on the other hand, looked nervous and stressed. She stretched her hand for a greeting.

"Mr. Michael Wright, Safiya Blue. I'm the owner. It's a pleasure to meet you."

His handshake was returned, but he held her hand a moment longer than normal. He ducked his head to the side for a second, shook her hand, and smiled. "I think we've met before. The farmers market, lemons and papaya.

*So, he remembered me.* She thought

"Yes. Every Saturday at nine a.m." They said in unison and laughed

On the other hand, the receptionist seemed to have be in la-la land. She couldn't stop gawking at the two of them.

"In fact. I just found out last night you won the bid hands down." He looked down at her shoes. When he finally brought his eyes to meet hers, he had a coy smile that troubled to her bodily reactions. He took a deep breath in and smiled like a boss.

Then reality sunk in. It made sense as to why he was upset after his phone the night before. She was sure he was into her at the market. Now that he knew she was his contractor/employee, with a strict no fraternizing with the employee rule, the game has definitely changed.

"We're also neighbors."

*That would explain why after the call he stared up at my condo. All while I masturbated and had an orgasm.* That thought brought a huge smile to her red glossed lips.

"Yes, we are."

Mike immediately got down to business. Setting up several rounds of individual meetings, a group lunch in the boardroom, and a congratulatory speech to the group on their many accomplishments, is how he introduced himself to the team. Safiya sensed Mike's cool, collected business practices were going to crumble when she got him alone in her office. She had wicked plans for him. Employee rules or not, she had to have a taste of him. She would bet her sweet round ass that for one night, he would let that rule slide.

Safiya walked past several empty offices. Usually, the receptionist was gone at five on the nose, but not this day. She was milling around the office. Mike had set up a makeshift office out of one of the vacant conference rooms. On numerous occasions throughout the day, they would touch or lock eyes and that set her soul ablaze. She could think of nothing more than her Red Woo lips wrapped around his throbbing dick.

She buzzed her receptionist. "Go home Meg. It's past five on a Friday. We're going to be a bit. Lock the entry when you go. Have a nice weekend."

There was a pause on the speakerphone from her receptionist, and then a bleak sad voice answered back. "Oh, All right. If Mr. Wright doesn't need me. I guess. Have a nice weekend."

Safiya knew that woman was hopeful, but she was certain nothing was going to happen between her receptionist and Mr. Wright. He hadn't taken a second look at her all day.

Several minutes passed, and Safiya leaned against her desk looking out of her door down the hall towards the conference room. Peeking her head in one more time, the receptionist tried to offer her expertise to Mike. Then she watched her sadly walk down the hall and wave good-bye.

With her legs crossed at the ankles, and her ass on the corner of her desk she was ready for production. Her black lace panties had long been removed.

A minute passed and Mike popped his head out of the conference room. He looked down the hall at her and saw her waiting. His smile deepened and his eyes undressed every inch of her. Safiya sat there with a come-hither look and let her red lips curve up into a sensual sexy smile.

She watched his swagger as he tried to walk all cool and collected down the hall. His pace quickened the closer he got. As soon as he was in her office, he closed her door and locked it. Safiya pushed off the desk and closed the window blinds. Once her office was closed for privacy, she turned to him, leaned her body into his, and whispered into his ear.

"Finally, a moment to ourselves. Would you like to have that one on one employee meeting now?" Her voice was sultry and indicative of sex.

As she loosened his tie and undid the first two buttons on his shirt, Mike cleared his throat.

"Relax." Safiya coaxed letting her fingers run over his shoulders. "It's been a long day. Come, sit, and take a load off."

She took his hand and led him to her leather office executive chair. She sat him down with a soft push of her hands to his chest. He fell back willingly. Now that she knew he was willing to let the employee relationship policy slide.

"How was your day?" She was bent over him with her hands on his knees. The valley of her breasts was pushing through her suit jacket. His look was intense and indecisive, so she decided she would make his mind up for him.

Bending her knees, she was now eye-level with the tent forming in his pants. He never responded and his breathing had become shallow. Mike's hand reached out and brushed her hair. "You are so fucking sexy. The first time I saw you at Ray's, I wanted you."

"I know." Her hands unbuttoned his shirt one button at a time. Reaching the top of his pants, he stopped her. He was hard. She felt it, and his breathing was labored.

"Safiya. That was until I found out for the next six weeks I will be your boss. Maybe we should stop now."

She laughed lightly. "Maybe we should, and maybe we shouldn't." She continued unbuckling his belt.

With her hands on the button of his slacks, he placed his strong hands firmly over hers. "Do you know how crazy I have been about you since our first meeting? I tried to get you out of my system. I asked Tiffany at the market, and she told me your name. My assistant found out the rest, inconveniently last night. Any other time, if we had met before I found out who you were..."

He let the insinuation linger and stared at her deeply. Now it all started to register and make sense to Safiya, All the familiar looking, tall, dark-haired beauties at his place were the figment of her.

"Why not just ask me out at Ray's?" Safiya inquired picking hand up and and laying it on the arm of the chair. She proceeded to unbutton and unzip his pants.

"It's complicated. I don't date, right now. Too busy with work."

The last part slowed her. Her tongue was already touching the tip of his erection. Her hand firmly grasped the base of his throbbing dick, and her mouth lay open with the tip of him poised to enter her mouth.

"Should I stop?" Not like she would, but she was teasing him with her eyes. His wood at her mouth, her suit jacket open exposing her black lace bra and her perky breasts.

Mike moaned and she took his fullness into her hot, wet mouth. She let him slide in and out of her moist mouth, letting the tip of rest on her tongue every so often. She ran her tongue around the tip and then deep throated his dick. She loved the weight and feel of his shaft, loved the thickness and the course of the vein that ran up the side. She licked his balls and he flinched for a second so she grasped firmly and shoved his whole dick down her throat again.

"God you're so fucking sexy right now. I can't believe how sexy you are." He moaned out. She sensed the tension beginning to build. He was holding back. She would have none of that.

"I love your dick." She licked the tip, grasped at the base of his glory again, and let her mouth create an incredibly tight suction on the top half. He flinched, tensed, and then shot his load in her mouth. Looking at his reaction, she swallowed each drop of his load. He pushed his head back then slowly lowered until their eyes met.

Her hand slid up and down and over the tip letting his cum cover every inch of his dick. His smile grew, and his hand reached out and pushed her hair off the collar of her suit jacket.

He moaned out her name. "Safiya?"

She knew the question and she had the answer, but not until after he returned the favor. She wanted his mouth on her pussy and him inside her. The moisture between her legs on her bare, wet pussy awaited his tongue.

Safiya put her fingers to his lips. "Shhh." She taunted slowly. She stood slowly, letting her suit jacket fall to the floor. Raising her skirt, she turned around and bent over her desk. She stood there momentarily, giving him an unadulterated view of what was underneath her skirt before pulling it down and stepping out of it. She stood before him in a black garter and black hose, knee-high black boots and a bra, but not for long. Reaching behind her back, she undid her bra and let it slid down her arms exposing her perky nipples and large breasts.

"Now, this meeting can officially begin."

She licked her lips and watched his pupils dilate. His smile deepened, he pushed up from the chair and stood. His pants dropped to the floor, and he stepped out of them. He still looked fucking sexy with his suit jacket and dress shirt open showing his bare and muscular chest. Stepping forward, she brushed her hands across his shoulders removing the remainder of his garments.

He took a step forward, and she took a step back. Two more steps and her ass met at the edge of her desk. She sat her round, firm ass on the mahogany desk and let her hands rest behind her for support.

Mike dropped to his knees and looked up at her. He looked as if he was ready to eat the buffet. She felt the lingering touch of his fingers inside her thigh and then between the wet folds of her bald pussy. Separating the lips, he licked at her clitoris once, then twice. His mouth went down and he created suction that shocked her out of her boots.

"Fuck!" Safiya screamed and tilted her head back. Her hand reached down and surfed the waves of hair before pulling him closer into her sweetest spot. His tongue lashed out, his fingers went in for a moment and then slid out. She could feel her body ready to convulse.

"Fuck me now." She begged.

With his fingers still in her, he stood and let his mouth assault her taut nipples. With tender kisses, he worked his mouth up to her neck and stopped just beneath her ear with tender kisses. She felt the throbbing of his manhood ready gain entry into her very wet pussy.

His fingers toyed with her clit for a second as her hands encased his hardness inside the lambskin sheath. His hand brushed over her hair.

"Safiya."

He said her name with sex to his voice. He guided his dick into her pussy. Her head tilted back again and the feel of his body pumping in and out of her was so incredible. Her moans were loud, and she felt his hand lay over her mouth gently as he whispered. "Shhh. Someone might hear us."

She nipped gently at his hand and then smiled coyly at him. "It's okay Baby cakes, everyone's gone."

His anxiety subsided and he let her have all he had to offer. He groaned a few times and pushed deep into her pussy. He firmly grasped her breasts and pinched at her nipples. She moved her hip forward just enough that he slid against her swollen clitoris and she was gone.

She tightened her pussy around his shaft. She felt small currents throughout her body. He pumped harder and faster. She was sure her tight, pulsating pussy was going to send him over the edge. He groaned loudly, his body tensed, he released and fell against her. She was flat on her back with one heel of her boot resting on his naked ass.

"Now, that's what I call a meeting." She joked.

They got themselves together and walked out of the office not exchanging much conversation. On the drive home, Safiya knew she had to take drastic action. Now that she had a feel of his dick, she would do whatever it takes to make this happen on a more regular basis, job or no job.

The next morning was Saturday and she didn't go to Ray's as she normally did. She was sure Mike got the email proposal she sent. Safiya offered to release the bid to the second highest bidder and work as a consultant to them. She wanted Mike more than ever and nothing would stand in the way of that. She had other clients and contracts, losing his wouldn't affect her business that much.

She was lounging around in a black tank top and a black thong, contemplating her day. She replayed the sex in her office over and over. She was sure Mike wanted more or maybe it was just the fact that she had her first taste of his sweet elixir and wanted to drink it all.

She saw him earlier stirring around in his loft. He stood facing her window with his boxers on drinking a cup of coffee shortly after wakening. He had one hand on the window, a huge smile on his face and a coffee cup in his other hand. Mike made a toast in her direction, but she knew he couldn't see her through her darkened windows. She stared at him, wondering why he hadn't called or emailed back. She had never let a man get this deep into her before. She always called all the shots.

It was past nine, and she hadn't seen him since he left his loft at ten to nine to go to Ray's market.

She poured herself a glass of orange juice and broke out the juicy strawberries she bought the night before. She took a sip of juice and was about to bite into a strawberry when her buzzer rang. She went over and pressed the button.

"Who is it?"

"Safiya. It's Michael Wright. Can I come up?"

She didn't answer, she buzzed him in. She was a little displeased he didn't call or email, but she didn't ponder on that. If he was there for sex she would give it to him because the sound of his voice made her wet. Realizing she didn't have on any clothes, she thought she should put on some shorts. She thought twice and figured that would just be more clothes to take off.

Once he got to her door, he noticed the door was unlocked and ajar. He pushed the door open with two hot coffees and a bag of pastries from Ray's.

"Safiya?"

"Over here."   She was straddling her chair with the juice of a strawberry dribbling down her chin.  She smiled at him coyly.

She watched him sit the food on the counter. His voice sounded nervous as he began to talk.  "I couldn't get you out of my mind last night.  I tossed and turned.  I got your email.  I..."

Taking another berry from the bowl beside her, she took a bite and traced her nipples with the open berry.  Mike placed the food and coffee on the table and walked to where Safiya sat.  She placed the remainder of the berry inside his open mouth.  She groped the tent inside his pants.  He flinched and was already hard.  Mike looked deep into her eyes and laid a kiss on her lips.  Before she could react any further, he had her in his arms. He kissed her mouth deeply with his tongue.  He pulled back and gently nipped at her lip. Then he pulled away when she did not react.

"Sorry."

"Don't be. I saw you last night. My room is directly across from yours. I saw your light come on, and you try to read. I watched you type away on your laptop. I masturbated at the thought of your dick in me and your mouth on my pussy and then I fell asleep."

Her directness shocked him for a second. He looked in the direction of his loft. The tinted windows dawned on him.

He quickly spoke up to reaffirm he wanted more with her. "I changed the policy about employee relations. I don't want you to leave. Your contract is secured with my company indefinitely." His voice sounded nervous and uncertain.

"What a relief for several of my employees. Two of them are planning fall weddings. I knew who you were the first time I met you at Ray's, otherwise I would have come on to you. I figured I should let you make that decision. I have no problems with it."

She eyed the coffees and bag of pastries then smiled. "Shall we eat?"

However, it was not the bag he grabbed, it was her waist. He brought her in close to his body and let his hands hang over her breasts, and between her legs where she was already wet.

She leaned forward letting the palms of her hands rest against the granite countertops in her kitchen. Her ass to rose in his direction. She looked over her shoulder and smiled at him.

"What I want to eat is not on that table over there!"

She didn't answer. Instead, she moaned at the feeling of his hard erection against her ass. He let his hand slide down around front and toyed with her clit. He pulled his hand away and practically ripped her thongs off. She gave him an instruction that he could not refuse with her in that position.

"Fuck me first Mike."

He didn't hesitate. He dropped his shorts around his ankles and was commando underneath. He grabbed his dick, tore open the condom from his pocket and slowly entered her tight wet pussy. He rocked in and out slowly letting the feel of her tight, wet pussy, and her moans of pleasure cause him to want to fuck her hard and fast. He watched her arch her back and he thrust in deeper and harder. He brought his hand up to her hair and removed the band that held her long, sleek, black hair. Her loud moans of pleasure caused him to cum fast and hard. He regretted the moment was over so fast. Mike wanted to spend the day with her doing the sexual things she had stirred within him since the first time they met.

As soon as the sensation subsided, he could tell she wasn't done. Safiya turned around and guided his hand across her clit and made his palm press hard and firm. She pushed hard up and down and then he let his fingers slid in just as her pussy tightened around them. He watched her scream out in pleasure while the palm of his hand held her slick bald pussy in it. It was a feeling of success for both of them and hopefully a feeling they could relive often.

They took a moment to collect their breaths. He still had his hand inside the front of her with her dripping wet. He decided to joke. "I need some substance now before I eat that sweet puss, let me feed you."

Her gentle laughter soothed him. She smiled with a look of a very satisfied woman. "Normally, I just go commando." Mike looked down at his shorts.

"I see you do as well. I was just wondering what to do with my day before you showed up. I can smell the cinnamon from that bag. I think we're going to have to work off the pastries you brought over later."

"Safiya? What did you decide?"

He could just eat her up with the way she was looking at him. He didn't want to lose his her company as the contractor because he couldn't keep his dick in his pants.

"I think we make a great team. Now feed me before I decide to eat you up."

She licked her lips and brushed her hand across his flaccid member. It flinched for a second and he smiled. However, his face in her pussy with her legs straddled over his face and her hot wet mouth sucking his dick, seemed to excite him. That position he couldn't get out of his head since they walked out of her office.

Something internally told him that she was game for whatever fun they would partake in. Her willingness made desire her more.

# House of Choo

There once was a maiden that lived in the house of Jimmy Choo. She had so many shoes she didn't know what to do. Her late husband, the consummate workaholic had no more love to spread. So while renovating her home, she decided to take the tradesman to bed...

When Wynda was 20, she imagined that at 35 she'd be happily married with a couple of children, and a great career. Well, things didn't work out that way. Instead, she spent years shopping and accumulating all the shoes she could while Parker Blackwell spread his love through the hood. Parker worked night and day, so Wynda's black card wouldn't be denied due to lack of pay. Wynda and Parker met while attending TSU. Their whirlwind romance ended the way many do, Parker died from

Viagra misuse, atop a harlot pretending to a real house wife too.

Wynda was a millionaire with too much time on her hands. She's turned into a walking cliché. That very put-together woman who spends her days between the gym and the beautician. Until she hatches a plan to have a romp with a handy man.

A few months ago Wynda decided to do something to connect with her former self, to be productive at last. She bought a run-down shack on the beach and moved in to do some of the renovating myself. Her friends thought she was crazy.

Soon Wynda fell into a soothing routine of painting, dealing with tradesman, and buying all the things she needed to make this little place heavenly. The pool was invitingly sparkly outside the kitchen window. The whole back of the house opened to the deck with an infinity edge pool overlooking the ocean. *The inside is finished and perfect,* Wynda thought to herself. There was still a large amount work to be done on the deck and Wynda couldn't wait until it was finished.

The last two builders working on her deck, Bryant, the fifty-five year old owner of Bryant and Son construction and Daemon who Wynda found incredibly attractive. When she opened the door to him the first time her breathing stopped when he smiled. He wasn't drop dead gorgeous, but when smiled, the world paused. He was wearing a paint-stained tee shirt and shorts that day and the muscles in his shoulders and arms were displayed beautifully. The magnificent abs were hidden, but her mind soon filled with a vision of him deliciously naked. He was lean, muscled, strong, and very, very sexy.

His eyes seemed to be suggesting things, and a secretive smile added to the idea he was naughty. Daemon awakened her that morning. Wynda stumbled to the door, sleep tousled, and hastily tying her robe.

∞∞∞∞Wynda∞∞∞∞

I'm not too good until I've had coffee, so it didn't register that one tit was fully exposed. The giveaway was in his amused expression and the direction of his gaze.

Looking down, I gulped to see my left breast exposed, nipple proud and pert in the chilly air. I cleared my throat, carefully re-adjusting my robe. "Oops," I said smiling sheepishly feeling my face flame.

He didn't rush to apologize. Instead, he stood there with a slight smirk, before drawling "I'm sorry for dragging you out of bed," and the way he said that made my toes curl. "I'm Daemon and Jamie's unloading the truck." He reached out to shake my hand. Instinctively, I met his hand with my own.

"I'm Wynda." His grip was firm and I could feel the calluses on his palm. He clasped both hands around mine, seemed about to lean in and say something else, before releasing my hands and getting all business like.

"Right then Wynda, we've got a deck to build, so I'll get to it. "

Since then, I spend plenty of time watching him work, and there's been a very surprising bonus. I'm horny again, and I mean, extremely, almost painfully aroused. It's Daemon, oh yes its Daemon. At first I'd position myself somewhere so that I could watch him work without being too obvious. I'd have a book in front of me and sunglasses on, but I'd be watching every move he makes. I've been salivating over his straining muscles, and secretly cheering when he removes his top and I get to see more.

I've been shocked at how frequently I've been masturbating. One particular day when Daemon was working close to my bedroom window, I decided to be very wicked indeed. I left the curtains open a crack. It turned me on to imagine Daemon glancing in and seeing me playing with myself. I wanted to fuck him. Oh, the boldness of that statement, that thought, made me so hot!

Since I made that decision my days were giddy with anticipation and fantasies. In my imagination I had him in every room of the house. He took me from behind, rough and unannounced. Oh, there were endless delicious variations. It was time to make one of them happen.

Careful to make the crack in the curtain not too wide, and extra careful to make sure Jamie wasn't any place close, I went back to the bed in nothing on but a pair of red lace and patent-leather open toed Jimmy Choo's on. The act of spreading my legs sent bolts of desire through me. He could look in and see my legs spread and my cunt inviting. He could come in and fuck me, stick his fingers in me, his tongue.

I only needed a little bit of pressure on my clit to be on the brink of orgasm, holding off the moment

I closed my eyes and pulled at my nipples, leaving my drenched, aching pussy alone for a bit. If Daemon looked in he'd be sure to get a hard on. My legs were spread wide and my fingers sped up. I was writhing, moaning a bit, lost in the sensations. I felt wild with lust, fearful and brave all at once. It was a heady combination I submitted to. I risked a look at the window from beneath my lashes and my heart nearly stopped when I saw Daemon's silhouette.

I hesitated for a minute and then continued, faster and more urgent than before. He was watching! My fingers worked faster and faster. The window was open and Daemon could hear the sound of my juices sloshing, my ragged breathing. When I came, I didn't hold back, I moaned deeply, long and loud, throwing my head back and pulsing over and over.

Slowly sliding my fingers free of my pussy; I left a wet trail across my stomach to my breast where I toyed with my nipples until they tingled in sensation. I smiled and sighed with deep satisfaction.

When I opened my eyes again the window was empty and I could hear hammering nearby.

*Things might be a little awkward now, or not*, I thought. I got dressed in my red halter top, black trimmed bikini and slinky red patent leather Choo's with four and half inch heel. I hatched another naughty plan.

It was almost 3 o'clock, close to the time the builders leave for the day. It was Friday and a little over 100°, what could be more natural than offering the boys a drink at the end of a hard week? Bryant wasn't likely to say yes. He had a regular Friday night dance class with his wife. Jamie had already left.

Trying to appear calm and casual I made my way out to the back deck and saw that I was just in time. Bryant and Daemon had almost finished packing up their gear. I couldn't help notice that both men gave me a once over as I approached. Bryant quickly averted his eyes, and the look Daemon gave me made it clear he was remembering what I did in my bedroom.

I hesitated a bit and felt my face heat up, but I found my voice. The invitation may have come out a little strained, but it wasn't too obvious. Raising a hand lower my sunglasses, I asked if they would like to stay for a drink. Bryant threw a quick look at Daemon then at me before clicking the lock on his toolbox and standing up.

"I'll have to pass, Zumba class with the wife tonight thanks Love."

He walked away passing close to Daemon ear and whispered, "You lucky bastard." He turned around the side of the house and disappeared.

"So," I raised a questioning eyebrow, "What about you? Can I offer you a beer, wine, spirit?"

Squinting against the sun, he said, "A cold beer would be fantastic, thanks. Do you mind if I clean up a bit?"

I was quick to offer him a towel, and the use of my shower. To my delight he agreed.

"I've got some clean clothes in the car, a shower, change of clothes and a beer sounds like heaven."

With that he headed off to his car to get his clothes. I went in the kitchen to pour a glass of wine for myself and grab a Heineken for Daemon. I wondered a bit at why he had a change of clothes so conveniently on hand. *Had he been planning a little seduction? Hmmm,* that was a warming thought. Oh yes, there was heat in all the right places. I already had two glasses by the time he returned smelling of citrus, mint and hint of cedar wood. I had time to dream up a few naughty little scenarios, and finally settled on the one that would get his hands on me the quickest.

I was reclining in one of the lounge chairs, and Daemon was sitting sideways on another lounge facing me. Leaning toward him for maximum cleavage I deliberately leant down and picked up the suntan lotion.

Rolling onto my front, I held the bottle toward him and asked, "Would you mind, I need another coat?"

"It would be my pleasure," he said smiling.

Laying back down on the recliner, I closed my eyes. An image of him standing in the window watching me play with myself almost made me moan with desire. There was the sound of the cap on the sunscreen opening, the squirt of liquid in his hands, and him rubbing the lotion in his palms. The thought of his hands touching me made my pulse increase.

I waited and nothing happened, about to lift my head I paused when Daemon asked in a husky voice, "Where would you like me to start?"

"Hmmm," I drawled, making the sound suggestive, sexual. "Hmmmmm, that's a hard decision." I repositioned myself on the towel, raised my ass a little and made it clap like I saw in the twerking videos. "How about start at the bottom and work to the top?"

Before I could finish the sentence his hands were circling my right ankle and slowly moving up. First he worked his way up in sensual circles and then he trailed his fingers down to begin the cycle again. Oh, how I longed for him to take those magic fingers higher. I wriggled again, hoping to encourage him to move straight to my pussy, to put me out of my misery. "Patience Mami," he said in a mock Spanish accent.

"Yo te voy a dar esta polla." (I'm gonna to give this dick.)

"Si, Papi" I replied. The look on his face indicated he didn't think I understood Spanish.

I wanted him fucking me soon. As though reading my mind, Daemon undid the bikini top, saying, "You don't want strap marks, do you?"

He slid his hands back down to the edge of my bikini and hooked a finger in each side. His breath was hot against my ear as he nibbled at my lobe. He slid my undies down my legs letting his fingers brush me in an erotic caress all the way down. Next, he moved to the end of the sun lounger and took an ankle in each hand. He separated my legs. Exposed on my stomach before him, I twisted my head to see what he was doing. He was staring at my cunt. I went with the urge to rise to my knees, paused enticingly for a moment before turning and lying down, face-up. Very deliberately, I then parted my legs nice and wide.

"I think you missed a spot," I said breathlessly.

His black eyes were filled with lust. He kneeled between my legs on the lounger and began unzipping his pants. The games were over now. It was time to get down to some serious fucking.

When he finally held his magnificent, engorged dick in his hand, I leaned forward and licked the tip and quickly laid back down, he groaned deep and long.

"You are one fucking dirty bitch, you know that? You wanted me to see you today didn't you?"

Using his knees his pushed my legs a little wider, and continued stroking the length of his dick. With his other hand, he reached down and slid a finger in and out of my ripe hole.

There was nothing but the sensation of his finger, taking me higher and higher. The sight of his straining muscles and piercing eyes did something to me. Almost screaming with the need for release, I gasped when he stepped back and took his fingers away.

In two quick motions, Daemon had a hand on the back of my neck. He forced his throbbing dick into my mouth. Through gritted teeth he demanded,

"Suck it, you filthy little whore. Suck me till I blow. Aaah, yes, ahhhh, you know how to suck dick, don't you, Bitch?"

No man had ever used language like that with me and my physical response was incredibly strong. I loved it, his words turned up the intensity, and when he did cum, I drank it down greedily. This was a first for me. Before, the idea of swallowing always turned me off, but this time it felt like what a dirty bitch would do. I felt slutty beyond limits.

Though he stood shaking and panting for a little while, it wasn't long before he straightened and gave me a wicked smile. "You suck dick very, very well Mrs. Blackwell. I just bet you're an excellent fuck too. Daemon's dick remained rigid and ready. He stood there in front of me proudly running a finger lazily over the base and up to the tip.

"Now my fingers felt a little wetness down there between your legs. What will we do about that?"

The sound that came out of me was more growl than voice "Fuck me now please, oh, please fuck me now."

Despite my pleading, he remained standing, playing with his dick and, looking at me.

He nodded towards my pussy, "Do you know what it was like this afternoon watching you fuck yourself from outside the window? I wanted to climb in that fucking window and screw your brains out. You didn't take long, you knew I was watching didn't you?"

"I knew you were watching," I answered. "I wanted you to climb in the window and fuck me. I want you inside me now. I'm so fucking wet you'll be up to your balls with one thrust."

That was all the encouragement he needed. He was between my legs, falling onto me and just as I said he was balls deep in one move. There was no need for fancy moves this time, I came after about three or four strokes. I came again not too long after that. He made me come five times that first Friday. That was a personal best for me. My handy man has a lot of work to do around the place these days. Bryant doesn't get out here much, and last time he did visit he made the point of saying, "The sort of work Daemon is doing really only needs one man, don't you think Mrs. B?"

I almost choked on my coffee before replying, "Daemon does a very good job, thanks Bryant. I have no complaints."

∞∞∞∞∞∞

There once was a maiden who loved some Jimmy Choo's. She brought so many she didn't know what to do. So she wore a new pair every time the handy man came around, he fucked her in every position, even upside down.

# STEAM BATH

Nasha rested her head against the wall of the sauna. The heat caused a sheen of sweat to glisten on her body. A moist bead slipped down her neck and rolled between her breasts. The sauna felt wonderful she thought as she felt her muscles relaxing. There was nothing like it after a vigorous aerobic workout. Marie kicked everyone's asses today. She would be sore for sure tomorrow.

The trainer who usually taught the class was definitely eye-candy. Chase was one of the reasons why she started taking the class. Chase had a body that would make your mouth water. It was toned and muscular, but not like a body builder's. His abs were well defined and the cut of his 'V' when he removed his shirt, made her tingle within her soft spot. His arms were toned, not an inch of fat on them or his legs. She wanted to wrap her legs around his body at least once. Chase was so damn fine. Nasha was growing wet just thinking about him.

She sighed and squirmed to try and lessen the discomfort that radiated within her pussy. She wanted Chase, but guys like him never looked twice at her. He wouldn't be interested in someone like her. Nasha didn't have a body like most of the women in the class, little waists and tight asses. She was a little overweight and needed to lose about fifty pounds technically seventy-five but fifty would do. She wasn't ugly and often received compliments on how pretty she was. Some people would often follow the compliment with "but you would be beautiful if you just lost some weight." It wasn't like she didn't know she needed to lose the weight, and she was working hard to make it happen.

Nasha wiped the irritating thoughts from her mind. She noticed the sauna had gotten hotter and what was sheen of sweat coating her skin minutes earlier were now droplets gliding down her body.

Twenty more minutes and it would be time to get out. Her body was so relaxed she felt like she could go to sleep. She inhaled and then exhaled slowly, closing her eyes breathing in the relaxation. She almost dozed off when she heard the door open and shut. Nasha peeked under her lids and her heart leapt into her chest, it was Marie and Chase.

Opening her eyes, Nasha sat up straighter and watched Marie take a seat down beside her. *Oh my God, Chase is so hot,* she thought. Marie wore nothing but a black sports bra and thin black Nike shorts. Nasha tried to keep from staring so she busied herself by pouring more water onto the hot rocks. Steam rose up and sizzled. It felt like the temperature rose another twenty degrees since Marie walked in.

"You did great in class today." Nasha jumped startled that Marie said something to her.

Composing herself she replied, "Thanks, you sure worked all of us hard in class today. I enjoyed getting my ass kicked by you though."

She heard Marie chuckle. "I enjoyed kicking your ass. It's great for the body sometimes to push boundaries, and I love keeping all of you on your toes."

Nasha smiled at her and it grew quiet. She hated the awkward silence that fell between them and she wanted to keep talking to her. So to make more conversation she said, "I think tomorrow I'm going to be sore. I can already feel it in my shoulders and arms. At least getting in here helps me somewhat."

Marie stared at her smiling. "I know what else helps sore muscles."

"What would that be?" Nasha asked.

She watched Marie scoot closer to her. Nasha felt her heart beat wildly in her chest.

"Squirting."

Nasha looked at Marie with a puzzled expression.

"Turn around, and I will show you." Marie instructed.

Nasha turned with her back facing Marie. She heard Marie snap her fingers twice and she felt a strong hand grip her neck, fingers pressing gently into her flesh. Chase massaged the back of Nasha's neck.

Those hands felt wonderful on her. Nasha couldn't believe what was happening. She often fantasized about this gorgeous instructor. She felt his hand move off her neck and disappointment washed over her. It was short lived, however, when she felt both of his hands grab her shoulders and began kneading her tight muscles. Nasha wanted to melt right then and there. She felt Chase slide his hands down her arms rubbing them gently. Nasha sighed and glanced at Marie. She could feel the hardness of Chase's body pressed into hers.

A hand gently grabbed her neck again and pushed it to one side. The fingers stopped their gentle assault on her neck, and warm lips replaced them. Nasha shivered and goose bumps arose along her skin. Her pussy was wet and ached. Nasha felt like she was in a dream. Kisses trailed down her neck to her shoulders. She felt Marie's warm breath along her skin. A warm feeling washed through her body and settled between her thighs. Her pussy ached like it never had before.

"Turn around," Chase whispered in her ear.

Nasha did as instructed. She turned and faced her.

"Drop your towel."

Nasha was conflicted. She was self-conscious about her body, but she didn't want to miss this one time opportunity to be fucked by Chase. She hesitated briefly and dropped her towel.

"Mmmm, so beautiful," Marie whispered as Nasha watched Chase dip his head down and take a nipple in his mouth. Nasha moaned and pulled Chase's mouth tighter to her breast.

"Oh yes Chase, suck it harder," Nasha begged. He complied.

Nasha tilted her head back and moaned in pleasure. She felt Chase grab her nipple between his teeth and then flick his tongue back and forth over the chocolate peak. His tongue lavished her nipple and his hand cupped her other breast squeezing it's nipple between his fingers and pulling gently. Nasha felt like she would orgasm just from the pleasure of her nipples being stimulated.

"Open your legs for me," Marie instructed while Chase continued to suckle her.

Nasha parted her legs. Chase pulled back from her breasts and looked down at Nasha's sex.

"Spread them wider. Marie stated. Let me look at that beautiful pussy."

No one had ever talked to Nasha that way. It turned her on. She wanted to please Marie too so she did as she was told and spread her legs wider.

"That's a good girl, so beautiful. I see your wetness. Your pussy is aching to be fucked."

Nasha whimpered. Marie's dirty talk was turning her on and Chase's hands were roving her body making her wetter. Marie watched Chase prop Nasha's feet on the bench, knees slightly bent. She grabbed Chase and pulled him closer, grabbing her legs and draping them over his shoulders. Marie watched as Chase parted her pussy lips. Oh yes, this was far better than any fantasy.

Chase ran his finger down to Nasha's hole, wetting it. He then ran it up and played with her clit.

Nasha's body jumped. Her pelvis moved in an up and down motion.

"Please, please, fuck me," Nasha begged.

She wanted Chase's fingers inside her, fucking her hard. Chase slid his middle finger in and then a second one.

"Oh God YES! Harder!" Nasha panted.

She felt Chase stop to insert a third finger. Nasha felt her vaginal walls stretch to accommodate all three of his fingers; she felt so full and tight. Chase's fingers felt incredible.

"You want him to fuck you hard, don't you?" Marie whispered in a sultry tone. Nasha could only shake her head.

"I want to hear you say it. Tell him to fuck your hard," Marie demanded stepping away from the two again so she could get a full view of what was transpiring.

"Please, Chase, fuck me harder." Nasha begged in a hoarse whisper.

She felt Chase pull his fingers out completely and then shoved them back inside her hard. Nasha arched her hips and thrust her hips in rhythm to Chase's fingers. He was pounding her so hard and fast. Nasha couldn't remember ever being fucked like this. She felt her vaginal walls tighten.

"Oh, not yet you don't darling," Nasha heard Chase withdrawing his fingers.

"I've been watching you in class and have wanted to do this to you since the first time I saw you. I want to taste your sweet pussy and finish finger fucking you."

Nasha couldn't believe what she was hearing. Chase wanted her too, her and not the other women with the tiny waists and perfect bodies. She lay on the bench and watched Chase lean down nestling his head between her thighs. Nasha propped up on her elbows to see. She saw Chase nuzzle his nose into her pussy lips. Nasha arched her hips up into his face. God knows she wanted to feel Chase's tongue licking her.

Chase parted Nasha's outer lips with his fingers and licked from Nasha's wet hole up to her clit. Nasha cried out in pleasure; her head spinning. Three fingers slid back inside her. Chase fucked her hard, pounding in and out of her drenched pussy. He finger fucked her and his tongue lashed across her clit.

"Oh fuck! You feel so good! Don't stop, make me cum!" Nasha begged preparing for the release that was building inside her.

"You taste so good Nasha. I could eat your pussy all day long," Chase said while his fingers fucked her.

Nasha felt her body climbing higher. She knew before long she would be coming. Chase withdrew his fingers completely and shoved them inside Nasha hard. At the same time he sucked Nasha's clit into her mouth. Nasha back arched and her legs quivered from her clit being sucked. The two different sensations were too much, Chase's fingers inside her, fucking her, and his mouth sucking her clit. She felt Chase thrust his fingers two more times before she went over the edge and sent the stream of liquid gushing from her pussy. Her body jumped and jerked as she screamed out Chase's name.

Nasha couldn't move for a few moments. Her body needed a few seconds to recover. She felt Chase trail his fingers from her breast to her mouth. Nasha shivered, sitting up. She looked at Chase and said, "That was incredible."

Chase leaned in and kissed her gently on the lip. Nasha could taste herself on him even more.

"You're everything I imagined you would be and more. Same time and same place next week,"

Marie said grabbing Chase and heading out of the sauna.

Nasha smiled and sighed to herself. Oh yeah, she would be there ready and willing. *It seems my workouts are going to become a lot more pleasurable,* she thought grabbing her towel and heading out of the sauna too.

# DeSiRe UnLeashed

Once again on a Friday night, Morgan Clark sat in her jetted tub allowing the jets shoot warm water against her soft spot imagining it was a man's tongue setting her on fire. Her orgasm hit her with its usual force and she let out a soft moan.

She pushed herself upright in the tub and added more hot water to the tepid water. Her mind drifted to the conversation she overheard between Felisha and Kelly in the office restroom. She was pretty sure they didn't realize she was in the stall around the corner and it probably wouldn't have made a difference if they had known.

"I bought me a new vibrating dildo last night," said Kelly.

"Did the old one quit working?" Felisha asked.

"No, I just needed an upgrade. This one ejaculates and it is eight inches long and 2 inches in diameter. It made me cum the first time I used it."

"Wow seriously, where did you get it?"

"I found it online at sextoys.com. I got a couple bullets and a new lubricant called Liquid Silk."

"I'm going online and order me some too."

The women exited the restroom and Morgan stayed put 'til she was sure the coast was clear. Thinking back on the conversation, she decided to go online and see what she could get.

She finished bathing, put her robe on, and headed for her computer. At twenty seven she was far from a virgin, but ever since the accident she became more of an old maid than she preferred. The remaining scars on her face and neck kept men at bay. Sitting at her computer, she typed in the site's name and her curiosity was instantly piqued. She ordered an ejaculating dildo and a suction dildo that she could use sitting on a chair. It was a little smaller than the ejaculating one, but it will serve its purpose.

By the time she was finished with her search she was hot and bothered again so she refilled her jetted tub and went another round with the jets on pulse. With her orgasm complete, she dried off and climbed into bed.

Two days later when her package arrived, she opened it with trembling fingers. Each item came with instructions on how to use them, how to clean them, and how to store them. The ejaculating dick came with recipes to make your own sweet sperm.

Anxious to try them out, she cleaned the curved dildo with the suction cup and placed it on one of her kitchen chairs. Taking some lubricant, she applied a liberal amount to the dildo, and stared at it in fascination. Surely it wouldn't all fit inside her.

Before trying it she removed her clothes and applied the nipple stimulators to her breasts. The suction and the gentle vibration tickled causing a slight giggle to escape her lips. She rubbed her thighs together and shivered. Next she applied some lubricant to herself before lowering onto the dildo. She took it in an inch at a time. She rose up and the sensation that whipped through her was heavenly. After two or three tries she decided to sit all the way down on it.

Feeling the width inside her and a slight sting she sat very still allowing her body to become comfortable with the dildo. Soon after she rocked back and forth on it and moaned at the exquisite sensation. Before long she was bouncing up and down on the thing until a powerful orgasm overtook her. The feelings she had been missing for years resurfaced as she pleasured herself.

The nipple stimulators were a bit uncomfortable and didn't compare to a man's mouth. When she pulled off her lovely dildo, panic set in. It was covered in blood, her blood, the proof her cherry had been busted.

She washed and sterilized the dildo. She studied the much larger ejaculating dildo and wondered if there could really be a man with a dick that size and if so how would one go about finding him. Considering how much the one she had just used filled her she wondered if she could get the bigger one inside her at all.

She decided to wait a few days before trying the 'Mandingo' on for size. She headed for the shower and a good night's sleep.

Five days later she thought she was ready for the 'Mandingo' as she called him. She had been using the suction cup one twice a night and figured she was broken in enough to use him. She ran hot water over the 'Mandingo' till he was nice and warm. She filled the reservoir with warm ejaculate fluid and climbed on her bed. Using a generous amount of lubricant, she touched the vibrating dildo to her clit and nearly fell off the bed.

Taking a firmer grip on the Mandingo she rubbed him all over clit, labia, and around her opening. When she could no longer stand it, she gently began inserting him into her creaming hot hole. He stretched her so much it was almost painful. It rubbed her insides with such exquisite deliciousness she wanted to cry and he wasn't even all the way in. She pulled him almost out and then shoved him back in a little farther. Her body shook with pleasure. She tried it again and this time she pushed him in as far as she could get him. Out and in, two more times and she climaxed. She held him in place until her insides stopped clenching.

Lying there, she turned the vibrator up to the next speed and let him rest deep inside her until the sensation built toward another orgasm. She thrust him in and out with a much greater speed and forcefulness. She reached her peak and pushed the bulb that made him spurt his cum as well. When the warm gush splattered against her cervix she went over the edge into oblivion.

Both 'Tiny', that's what she called her suction cup dildo, and 'Mandingo' became a nightly addiction. When she got home she changed out of her work clothes into a short nightie, impaled herself on 'Tiny' while she read her mail, slowly rocking back and forth till she climaxed. After dinner she headed for her bedroom to enjoy 'Mandingo'.

With 'Mandingo' she enjoyed prolonged sex play, moving him ever so slowly all over her body, across her clit and in and out of the entrance to her hole. When she couldn't put her orgasm off any longer she plunged him in as far as he would go and as fast as she could move her hand until she was moaning her climax.

One time she shut off the vibrator, left him in place and fell asleep. When her alarm went off she tried to remove 'big guy' but the sensation of sliding him out made her push him back in. The vibrations swept through her turning her on. She turned the vibrator on high. She had never used the highest setting before and it had her creaming in minutes.

When she arrived at her office everyone seemed just a little happier, and complemented her on her glow and smile. The smile never left her face all morning. People started to notice she was losing weight. She wasn't eating as much because she spent all her time at home getting her rocks off. After work, she was going to order a shower dildo so she could try it with water running over her sensitive skin. She was rapidly becoming a little sex fiend.

The day her shower toy arrived she couldn't wait till bedtime to shower and give it a try. This one had G-spot stimulator on the tip. Adjusting it to the right height took her some time, but once she had it just right she impaled herself on it, turned the water on, and started having the time of her life. The hot water sluicing down over skin felt like warm silk. She raised her breasts up toward the shower head and her nipples turned to hard little pebbles while the streams pulsated over them increasing her pleasure.

She moved her hips back and forth slowly at first, but the G-spot stimulator made her go faster and faster. She couldn't slow down if she wanted to and Lord knows she didn't really want to. When she came she came hard. She screamed and slapped the tiled wall of the shower with her hands several times. Moaning, she slipped off of the dildo and sunk to the bottom of the shower. Her pussy pulsed and her breathing was erratic. She pressed her hand against her pussy and squeezed her legs together. It took a whole minute before she was able to stand and finish her shower.

∞∞∞∞∞∞

Stepping out of the shower, her doorbell rang several times. Whoever was on the other side of the door was so insistent. She slipped on her robe and went to answer it with dripping hair. She opened the door a crack and there stood an incredibly handsome man in oversized Nike shorts and black wife beater. His eyes looked worried.

"Are you all right?" he asked. His head was bald and shiny with perspiration.

"I'm fine. Why do you ask?"

"I heard you scream and then I heard a loud thud. I thought perhaps you had fallen or someone was doing you harm. Are you sure you're okay." Words from his wide mouth and full lips flowed over her like warm maple syrup.

"Oh," she felt her cheeks grow hot, "No I'm fine, really."

"I just moved in next door, my name is Craig but everybody calls me Slim. If you ever need anything just call on me."

She could tell by the tone of his voice he didn't believe her. She was sure if he knew the real reason why she screamed and slapped the wall he would laugh at her or worse yet feel sorry for her.

"I'm Morgan, and I assure you there is nothing to worry about. Now, if you will excuse me I need to go dry my hair."

"Of course, but remember if you need HELP I'm right next door." She closed the door and leaned against it. *Dear God, how embarrassing. I have to be more careful, I forgot how thin the walls are here.*

Even though the handsome man god wasn't still standing in front of her, her face flamed at having been heard through the walls. Morgan moved into the bathroom and dried her light brown curls. She glanced over at her shower and groaned, her dildo was still stuck firmly to the tiles. She decided not to remove it because it took her so long to get it in just the right place, and she definitely planned to use it again, but she would be quiet about it. Maybe she needed to order one of those ball gags she saw on the website.

The next time she ran into her neighbor both of them were carrying bags of groceries. She nodded a greeting, hurriedly unlocked her door, and slipped inside. A few moments later her doorbell rang.

She opened the door a crack and there stood Craig. "Hi Morgan, I was wondering if you would like to have dinner with me tonight. I'm making my famous lasagna."

Morgan was speechless; no man had ever invited her to dinner, none, zero, and zilch. She wanted to say yes, but couldn't find her voice to do so. He must think her silly. He raised his eyebrows expectantly waiting for her reply. Finally finding her voice she said, "I'd love to."

"Good, come over in half an hour." He turned to go then spun back around. "Do you drink wine?" She nodded in the affirmative.

She leaned her forehead against the closed door and sighed. Every time she used her toys lately she imagined it was Craig making love to her. Her fantasy would never come true, but it didn't stop her from dreaming it could, and now he asked her to have dinner with him.

She stood before the mirror in her bathroom trying to decide whether to wear her hair up or down. Up showed her scars more. She knew one hour was not enough time to shampoo and blow dry her hair, so she pulled it back and tied it at the nape of her neck. What the heck he might as well let him see all her scars.

She rang his bell and he greeted her at the door with a glass of wine. "Hi, I hope you like Pinot Noir."

She smiled at Craig as he handed her a glass of red wine. He pulled her inside his apartment. She took a sip of the wine before answering him.

"Delicious, I like it very much." He looked wonderful in his faded jeans and chocolate V-neck sweater.

∞∞∞∞∞∞

Craig Mack listened intently every night for a week. He heard moans coming from his neighbor's bedroom. It only took him a couple of nights before he realized the sounds he heard were the cries of a woman in climax. However, he knew she lived alone so he figured she had to have been masturbating.

He would love to give her the real thing, but wasn't sure she would accept him. Her scars didn't matter to him. He had a few of his own. Shy and somewhat antisocial as she appeared to be, he wanted to be the one to bring her out of it and see her in the throes of an orgasm, especially one delivered by him.

Listening to her every night in the throes of ecstasy made him long to give her what she needed. Ultimately, he would end up in a cold shower or jacking himself off, which to him wasn't very satisfying. He wanted to bless her with his gift and bring her to culmination. Tonight he would begin his seduction of the sweet little miss.

Craig poured a glass of wine to hand to her at the door. Hopefully after a few glasses she might be acquiescent to a little sex play. He decided to play it as he went to see how receptive she might be. He already had vivid images of her love faces in his head, from listening to her voice.

His doorbell chimed just as he began to readjust his member to a more comfortable position. The task completed he picked up the glass and opened the door. She looked amazing standing on the other side of the door, in a currant cowl neck top, knee high boots and black skirt. He picked up his own glass and escorted her to the sofa.

"Dinner will be ready in ten minutes. I thought we could take this time to get acquainted with each other. How long have you lived next door?" He sipped his wine and awaited her answer.

"I transferred here six years ago from Gary, Indiana. I work in the HR department of Fuji Oil. What about you?"

"As you know I moved in two weeks ago, my grandmother left me this apartment in her will. I used to live across town, but this is closer to my work so I decided to move into it." They conversed for a few more minutes and then the timer on his oven went off.

Craig took the food from the oven and set it on a trivet on the table. He asked her what kind of dressing she preferred on her salad.

"Raspberry vinaigrette or balsamic are my favorites, but Ranch will suffice." She walked into the kitchen as she spoke.

"I happen to have those on hand, I love the lighter taste." Craig reached into the fridge and pulled out the traditional balsamic and strawberries because he knew it went best with the lasagna. He sprinkled it over the greens and tossed the salad.

"Thank you for coming on such short notice; it really is no fun eating alone. That's the main reason I eat out a lot. There are always people around even if you don't talk to them you can still hear them and know you are not alone." He watched as she licked her perfect lips. The tip of her tongue, swept over her upper lip, and he thought of sucking it into his mouth.

"I understand completely." She replied as she brought another forkful of food to her mouth. He imagined thrusting his tongue into her hot little mouth. Blood surged to his groin and his manhood started to swell even more. He shook his head and started shoving his own food into his mouth.

She had perfect white teeth and smooth caramel skin that told him she took good care of herself and practiced good hygiene. It said a lot about the kind of person she was and also about the kind of lover she would be willing to accept.

Every time she looked down at her food he refilled her wine glass. He didn't want her drunk, just slightly loose, free to be herself. He wanted her to be aware and looking into his eyes when she reached her climax.

His member was so hard it hurt. He reached down into his lap and stroked it a little, hoping to make it feel better, but it didn't work. All it did was make it difficult to concentrate on anything else. He needed to stop looking at her, stop thinking about the sounds her lovely mouth made over and over.

He pushed his empty plate back and poured himself another glass of wine, think about something mundane. "Do you have a favorite dish you like to cook?"

"Actually I have several, but I don't cook them very often because I have no one to share them with, and I get tired of the leftovers. I used to make a couple of things and freeze them in small containers to eat later, but most of them ended up with freezer burn so I eventually threw them out. I decided it wasn't worth it." She laid her fork down on her plate. "The only one I never throw out is macaroni and cheese. I could eat that every day."

They both smiled. He got up to clear the table and she got up to help him. His sex organ was nearly back to normal, he was thanking God for that.

∞∞∞∞∞∞

Morgan felt completely at ease with Craig. His charm and easy manner made her feel quite safe and secure. She was aware he studied her while they ate; she was used to people looking at her because of her scars so it didn't bother her. Years of dealing with people staring can toughen one up.

While she was helping him clean up the dishes, she noticed how long and thick his fingers were. He had very short, neatly trimmed nails. She imagined those fingers shoved into her sex and she suddenly felt warm all over.

Deciding it must be the wine, she tried looking somewhere else and her gaze settled on his sensuous mouth. She had the strongest urge to kiss his lips, to feel his arms around her, holding her close. Would he kiss her? Should she kiss him? Remembering her scars, she did nothing. He probably felt sorry for her; that's why he invited her to dinner. *Kindness is all it is*, she thought.

When she got back to her place 'Mandingo' would get a real workout and she would pretend it was Craig. After the dishes were done and I put away, they took their wine and sat on the sofa. Gazing into her eyes, Craig took her hand in his and brought her fingers to his mouth and kissed the tips. He sucked the middle finger into his mouth holding her rapt attention.

She went from cold to blazing in two point two seconds, literally. She experienced a warm moisture in her panties. She didn't pull away; she stared into his eyes mesmerized. The spell broke when he took her face in his hands to kiss her. Panic set in and she tried to pull away, but he didn't release her. His warm mouth descended on hers with tender gentle massaging movements.

His kiss sent vibrations shivering down her spine, her breath was caught in her throat, and her nipples tingled. His tongue swept over her lower lip and when she opened her mouth he plunged inside. She dropped her nervousness and wrapped her arms around his neck.

When he sucked her tongue into his mouth she whimpered in the back of her throat, her nipples hardened some more. His teeth caught her lower lip in a sensuous tender scrape as the kiss ended. She wanted to beg him to leave his mouth glued to hers, but was too unsure of herself to ask it.

He lifted his lips and whispered against her mouth. "I've wanted to do this since I first saw you peeking through your door soaking wet in a soft robe so sweet looking."

His finger trailed down her chest and over an already peaked nipple, sending fire to her pussy. "These," he continued, "Were budded and pushing against the fabric of your robe. I so wanted to take them into my mouth and suck them." He kissed her nipple through her clothes and she let out a soft moan and her panties got wetter.

*Could this really be happening to her?* Could this gorgeous hunk really want to make love to her, scars and all or was he playing her. At the moment she didn't really care as long as he continued to caress her.

His mouth left her breast and travelled up her neck, his hand traveled up her leg massaging her thigh and finding its way to her panties. His finger pushed aside the fabric of her panties and touched her sex. She held her breath in anticipation. He brushed his finger back and forth over her slit then dipped inside to gently massage her opening.

Morgan was floating outside herself. The sensations felt so good, she let her inhibitions flee. *Go inside, go inside*, she prayed, and he did. She nearly climaxed with him pushing his finger deeper into her creaming canal. Instinctively, she reached for his dick and was rewarded with his groan. He was so hard and so big. She wanted him inside her taking her to heavenly ecstasy. His finger rotated inside her and made her bold.

She unzipped his pants and pulled his engorged member from his boxers. Her hand slid over the smooth swollen head and found it slick with precum. She wrapped her fingers around him and squeezed. He thrust in her hand. Holding the real thing beat everything she had experienced to date. Erotic, salacious, sensuous, these words flashed her mind as she held his velvety rock hard erection in her tightly fisted hand.

He stood, picked her up, and carried her to his bed where he undressed her and started kissing her body all over. His mouth traced one of her scars sending shivers down her spine. Making love was nothing like fucking oneself with a dildo.

She pulled his shirt out of his jeans and ran her hands up his back. It was then she felt the puckered flesh and ridge of a scars that ran the length of his back. Like her he was damaged goods. She was too far gone to care.

Her hands pushed his pants down and she squeezed fingers into his ass cheeks. His mouth worked its magic on her nipples as he alternately licked and sucked them into his fiery mouth. Shocks of desire swiftly swept from her breasts directly to her pussy and it wept. Her hips moved of their own accord up and down.

He swiftly divested himself of the remainder of his clothes and covered her body with his. He nudged her legs apart, slipped on a condom, and positioned his erection at her entrance. She wanted this more than anything. The insides of her pussy were quivering in anticipation and she thrust her hips up trying to push him in. He pulled back away from her wetness and looked into her eyes.

Holding her face in his big hands he said. "Morgan, look at me. What's my name?"

"Craig" she breathed out breathlessly.

"Do you want me?" He asked.

Morgan closed her eyes and nodded.

Craig took her face in his hands, "I want to see your eyes as I enter you for the first time. I want to see the pleasure in your eyes when I make you cum."

She moaned her reply unable to speak any coherent words.

His passion filled eyes looked directly into hers as he slowly stretched her, filling her with delicious tension. Pleasure rippled from deep inside her and spread along her nerve endings. He pulled back and thrust in again, this time a little deeper touching something so exquisite she cried out.

"Did I hurt you?"

"No, oh no it's so good, so good." She kept her eyes locked on his even though she wanted to close them and drown in the feel of him as he moved in and out slowly.

"You are so tight, you make me want to cum right now," he whispered reaching between their bodies to press on her clit. He made little circles over the sensitive nub causing her insides to contract. Every muscle in her body was strung tight as a bow, when they began to quiver she felt like she could fly.

"Oh God," she whimpered, "I think I'm coming."

Immediately he began slamming into her sweltering pussy taking them both over the edge into to mindless pleasure. He didn't withdraw immediately; he stayed with his body resting on top of hers.

He was kissing the side of her neck and nibbling softly with his breath hot on her skin. She basked in the revelation she had what other women did, a real man with his hot hard dick deep inside her bringing her to a climax. It went far beyond her wildest imaginings. Far better than any of her toys.

Craig rolled off of her and pulled her into his arms, "Stay with me, let me love you again, let me hold you all night. I need you and you have no idea how much I need you. I want to be inside you again taking you with me into sweet ecstasy."

"Craig, I want it too. I never thought I'd have a man deep inside me. I love what you did to me, for me." Her hand caressed his chest, her finger swirling around his nipple.

"Why didn't you tell me you were a virgin? I would have gone slower."

"Because I'm not technically a virgin, I was taken forcefully years ago in high school. You're the first man to ever pay any attention to me. I never had another sexual experience with a man. A couple months ago I embarked on self-pleasure. If I had known what I know now I would have saved it for you."

He kissed her deeply, his tongue caressing the insides of her cheeks, skimming over her teeth and stabbing deep into her mouth. His fingers found her nipple rolled it into a hard little bud sending streaks of desire right into the center of her pussy.

"Technically, you were a virgin since I'm your first real man. I've just been where no other man has. I'm staking my claim on you right now." His mouth clamped on to her nipple and he sucked it hard making her pussy ache with even greater need to be filled all over again.

His hand covered her mound as a finger pressed against her sensitive core making her writhe against it. His erect shaft rubbed against her thigh. Craig kept it up 'til she cried out begging him to take her again.

"Please, please," she begged, "I can't stand it any longer. I need you inside me now."

Everything between her legs burned with the need to be quenched. He put on a fresh condom, flipped her over, pulled her hips up in the air and entered her from behind. She clasped her pussy tightly around his rock hard shaft. She almost came on his first thrust. Her breath came in short pants. She felt the wetness on her face and she pushed back against his magnificent member.

Craig gave her words of encouragement saying, "That's it babe, that's it. Push back hard, give me all of yourself." His thrusts were measured and hard. When Morgan came, she came so hard she could do nothing but cry. Her canal did spasm after spasm as he pumped faster and faster till he stiffened then collapsed against her back. When he pulled out her vagina was still throbbing.

No matter what happened in the days to come she would have this night to remember she would let him fuck her as often as he wanted all night long.

They lay spooning to rest a bit when he asked the question she knew would be asked eventually.

"How did you get burned?" He knew they were burn scars because he had some also all down one side of his back.

"When I was fifteen, I ran through fire to help save my momma. They used to be worse but I had some surgery and there are a lot less of them now. And you?"

"A girlfriend burned me with scalding hot water after I caught her in bed with another man. We argued in the kitchen and when I turned to leave she threw the pot on me. Had I been wearing more than a t-shirt it probably wouldn't have been so bad."

"Craig, if you weren't scared would you have still wanted me." His hand on her breast tightened, and he kissed her shoulder.

"Yes, but I didn't know you had them when I first desired you. Then after I saw you, I felt safer with you because I knew you wouldn't reject me because of mine." He brushed the pads of his fingers over her nipple and it puckered in response.

"I take it you have been rejected by women before." she turned in his arms and kissed his collarbone.

"Many times, no one seems to understand that scars are on the surface, not inside us. They don't define who we really are."

It warmed her heart to hear him say something she thought all her life. She moved her kisses down his chest to his nipple and ran the tip of her tongue around it and over it. She found it surprising his nipples responded the same way hers did. Morgan pursed her lips over the tight tiny nub and gently sucked. His body jerked. Warmth flooded her sex. He rolled to his back taking her with him. She stretched out along his form and continued to suckle at his nipples.

His erection poked at her nether lips and she opened her legs for him slightly so he could rub between those lips. The skin to skin contact of his dick plowing through her pussy lips sent a shock wave of delight through her. He pulled her up his chest and she whimpered at the loss of contact with his shaft.

"Ride me sweet one. Now rise up a little." She saw the head of his dick peeking from her trimmed bush, dripping moisture onto his belly. "Now slide back and forth." She did and he groaned. "Now make us cum."

She rode him slowly at first savoring the feel of him as she rubbed the length of his erection between her swollen labia. The corona rubbed her clit sending electricity through her body. His hands were massaging her breasts. She moved faster and faster over his hardness. She came with blinding speed, but he hadn't yet.

"Move slow babe, so you can feel me cum."

The experience of his ejaculation moving up the tube along the underside of his shaft caused her to have another orgasm. His cum squirted onto his belly and she tried to catch it with her fingers. It was hot. She put her cum covered finger in her mouth so she could taste him. Salty and a tiny bit bitter, his white essence caught her imagination and she shivered.

"Can I taste you?" she asked.

He smiled at her. "All you want my sweet, all you want, as long as you let me taste you as well." She bent over and licked the length of him and then took his softening member into her mouth and sucked. He tasted so good, slightly bitter sweet.

When they were through they showered together and went back to bed hopefully to sleep in each other's arms.

"Morgan, the night I came to your door, did you slip and fall in the shower?"

She gave a heavy sigh, "No, I didn't fall and I was experimenting with making a bit of pleasure of my own." She didn't want to tell him about the dildo stuck to the shower wall. Her face grew warm at the thought of him knowing about it.

"I thought so. I've heard your moaning before, but tried to keep it out of my mind...I'd like to make you scream like that."

"Oh, Craig, you've already done one better than that. You brought tears of joy and untold pleasure to my eyes. I was so overcome I couldn't even scream." Her hand caressed his cheek as she spoke. She could so easily fall in love with him. She snuggled into his body. Life would change for the better now she had a man to make love to her instead of a piece of plastic.

"Craig, will we do this again sometime?"

"Every day if you want."

She wanted all right, every day, twice a day or more. As often as he would take her.

# Erotic Poetry Table of Contents

# Her Inner M♥St

There is but one

Thing she desires most:

She needs to tease and be teased,

She adores to please and be pleased,

The anticipation of a slowly building up

To a sweet release.

Is so satisfying,

Bringing such a pleasurable release,

So draining,

So desirable.

This is her inner most desire.

Would you like to lie with me

On the floor?

An intimate coupling between

Friends and lovers

Colliding and sliding

Many passionate embraces

That would please me

Would that please you?

# Incredible Addiction

I am struggling with addiction every day,

Trying to detox by remaining away.

I want to feel it all the time,

I wake up in the morning with you on my mind.

Craving your high all day through,

Why can't I ever seem to get enough of you.

I realize this problem is oh so wrong,

It's hard to kick a habit I've had it so long.

A few days go by & I'm doing pretty good,

For without you,

I will go as long as I could.

Then you come back, drawing me in,

And once more we're at it again.

Repeating to myself, "just one last time,"

One more taste and I'll be just fine

Relapse, relapse damn I've lost control,

Breathless moments have seized my soul

Take me over, do what you will,

Fuck me faster, work those skills

This addiction isn't what you thought,

It's you...

that dick...

and the way you fuck me

with everything you've got!

# He Loves Her Sway...

I love to watch your sexy ass

As we walk down the street

I can't walk in front

or even beside

I need to follow behind with roaming eyes

so I can watch the way your sexy ass sway

the motion of your hips from

to the left then to the right

Stroll on my love, it's a glorious sight

With my fingers in my pocket

Dance across my member

Only to your rhythm

Passersby wonder about my joy

The vision before me brings out the little boy

Home at last,

you stand before me naked

Stilettos on, sway across the room

It takes everything I have not squeeze

those sexy bare ass cheeks

Walk past me once more please

# Acts ♡f Congress

Encase me against the cold frosted glass.

Grasp my breast, give me a spank on the ass

Pinch my nipples, let them twinge and stand so proud..

Whispering loving sentiments in my ear

of the love we found

Enter me with your golden stick

You make me wet, so quick

Caught up in sensations to the floor we tumble. .

Never releasing our hold, our love won't fumble.

Pressing in deeper and harder you ride

I'm flying high like a newlywed bride

We climax together still gasping for air.

Unmoving like statues chiseled so fair

If someone were watching

our love would be plain to see

These acts of congress are wonderful to me

We smile and gaze at each other

Knowing at this moment there will never be another

# The Aftermath

He enjoyed the tender moments

After the tormenting storm

almost as much as the tempest

herself

He laid immobile while she

lay prone and exerted upon him

her head dampened upon

his chest.

Just like the calm after the storm

He enjoyed her like this

Soft, submissive and worn

His hands absentmindedly stroked her

curves, his lips brushed

her frontal lobe

He fell under her spell

bemused,

bewitched.

He was convinced that his

Soul she now possessed

Death couldn't limit their time.

If she were called at eight He'd go at nine

He felt his member stir

Between the softness of her fur.

His appetite for

her was seemingly insatiable.

Would he ever get enough of her zest

Doubtful at best

He kissed her slowly

possessively deeply leaving her in

no doubt that;

she is his lost rib

…the only one he ever wanted

…the only one he ever will

# ♥ Training Day

He wanted to come over to test the waters

He said he's been chasing for that exquisite nut

I told him to start by making lip locking love to my clit

Slowly lap it up like a melting cone

Suck it, lick every drop likes it's been that long

Take one finger then two,

don't miss a beat in this rhythmic screw

To become one with her mold, caress every fold

Just pounding the beast to an unknown beat

Is not the way to appreciate her precious meat

Anticipation is the key to unlock her flow

Lessen the urgency, take your time go slow

Make her anticipate that nut

Flip positions if you must,

Long steady strokes

Rocket it baby,

Rocket baby like riding a boat

Increase the stride, smooth shifting gears of fly ride

Get ready for the explosion

As your bodies collide in the ultimate convulsions

This lesson is almost complete

When the eruption between ova and sperm

…greet between the sheath

# Untitled..

I lost my mind after the taste

Dazed, my head began to sway

Your hands on my body

bones begin to scream, I

wanna mix my beauty with

your beast

Mix our cream till we cease

Feel my soul seep all around

You're just what I need,

You've

filled my greed

I wanna watch you burst

and glisten with love

My Ruby Woo lips,

trace your ink

Our hearts are burning

Let our colors collide,

breathe out my name in one

lustful groan

# My Love

You're standing there

before me

Glistening, beautiful and wet

Your essence floats high above

Surrounding your body in a glow of love

The feel of your body over mine

So close we become one

Interlocked in everlasting flame

Swapping souls has never felt the same

Hold me close

Kiss me,

touch me,

tenderly

Your fingers run through my hair

Into your soul my heart stares

Angels scribed our name in the stars

My love, My soul

# My Fire

Your silky chocolate frame

Glazed by the sensuous kiss of the moon

Illuminating the contours of your body

While embracing all of its curves

Beads of sweat sparkle like diamonds and

Dance with delight

Soft whispers and sweet songs tantalize

Two voices become one in an unwritten melody

With every glance you give me fever, I ache for you

I can hardly stand when you look at me so

sensually

I cannot resist your embrace

So gentle and powerful that a single touch

Of your hands burns deep in my soul

With every breath I take my knees become weak

I am yours, I succumb to your electricity

You arouse my senses with tender kisses upon my back
and breast

My thighs quiver from the way your tongue explores
and taste

The things you do to me makes my blood

Run through my body like liquid fire

# Seduction

Seduction is a mighty word,

As powerful as you've ever heard,

Let me whisper in your ear,

Starting out with a simple glance,

Doesn't end after I'm in your pants,

Telling you everything you want to hear,

Let me whisper it in your ear

I can calm your every fear,

As I gradually get into your head,

You'll beg me to take you to bed.

Seduction is my mighty tool,

Whispers can make you act like a fool,

More powerful than any drink,

My whispers give no time to think,

Pretty soon time will tell,

If my whispers put you under my spell,

Yeah, My seduction is a mighty word,

My whispers of seduction the sweetest you ever heard

# Passi♡nately...

We're moanin' and groanin'

Been lickin' and kissin'

You're pushin' and I'm shovin'

Yet we ain't Fuckin'

We lovin' and huggin'

Suckin' and Touchin'

You're wantin' and I'm waitin'

And we ain't even Fuckin'

Our passionate anticipation

We're waitin' and wantin'

Wantin' copulation

No More waitin'…

No More wantin'…

*LaRedeaux*

It's Lovin' and Gropin'

AND PASSIONATELY FUCKIN

Is there anything better?

# Dark Side...

I need to love you

In dangerous ways

Bearing our intimacies

Unscrupulous intentions

Riveting intense

Pleasures of sin

Our fantasies freed

Filled with uninhibited

Acts unscripted

Fornication unleashing

Unashamed demons

Pure desire

Appeasing sexually

Untamed urges

Where darkness resides

*LaRedeaux*